A MAID, TWO DREAMS, THREE IS A CROWD

Annabella Baker

Copyright © Annabella Baker 2022

The right of Annabella Baker to be identified as the author of this work has been asserted following the copyright, Designs, and Patents Act.

All right reserved. No part of this publication may be reproduced, transmitted, or stored in a retrieval system in any form or by any means without the permission in writing from the copyright owner, nor otherwise circulated in any form of binding or cover other than that in which it is published and without a similar condition being imposed on the subsequent purchaser.

This is a work of fiction. All characters in this publication are fictitious, and any resemblance to real people, alive or dead, is purely coincidental.

"Sugarcane is always sweet. People only sometimes so."

Myanmar Proverb

Of the same author:

GLOOMY SUMMER, 2022

LETTER FROM TEPLICE, 2022

DINNER AT THE PENINSULA, 2023

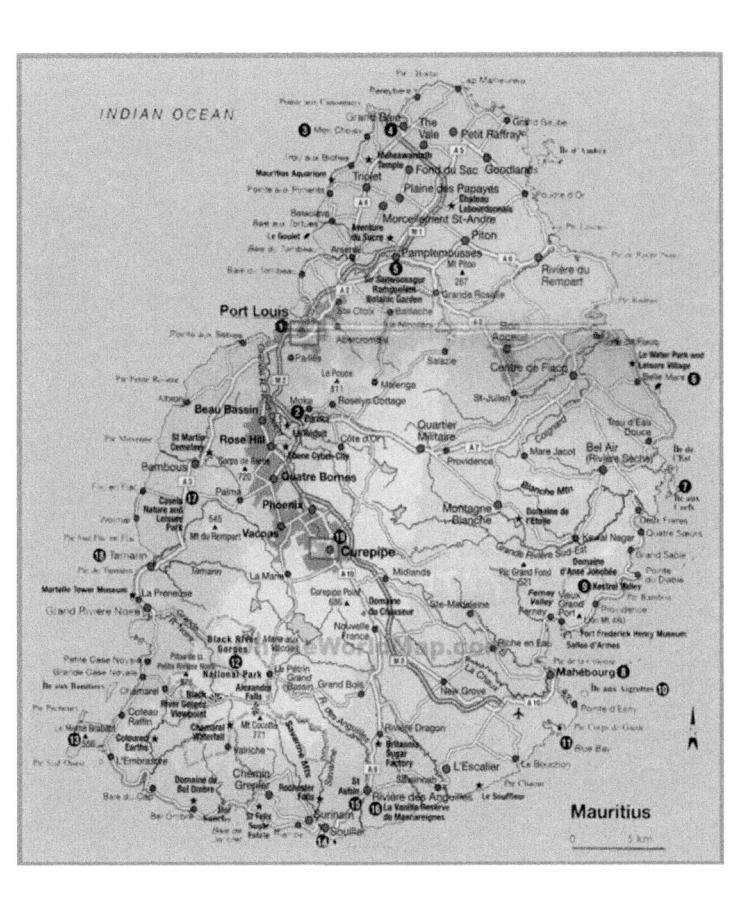

TABLE OF CONTENTS

CHAPTER ONE *1*

CHAPTER TWO *17*

CHAPTER THREE *35*

CHAPTER FOUR *45*

CHAPTER FIVE *57*

CHAPTER SIX *63*

CHAPTER SEVEN *73*

CHAPTER EIGHT *89*

CHAPTER NINE *105*

CHAPTER TEN *123*

EPILOGUE *135*

Chapter 1

"Ce Pays cultive la canne à sucre et les préjugés."
"This Country cultivates sugarcane and prejudices."
-Malcolm de Chazal, "Petrusmok"

"Don't forget we will be twenty-four at dinner tonight, and I expect the best as usual."

"Oui Monsieur Henri".

"I need my pink shirt ironed and ready", he raised his voice to make sure he would be heard from the veranda.

"Oui Monsieur Henri".

Henri nodded once and Mareva left the room.

Mareva was used to his voice but for Nicole her husband's voice made her always startle and again today his harsh voice caused the book in Nicole's hand to drop on the gleaming marble floor. She looked up at him from across the wide living room.

Nicole's eyes followed their maid retreating until she was out of sight. When she looked back at her husband, his steely gaze was now trained on her face.

"Do not embarrass me tonight."

"Yes Henri."

"Make sure you will be wearing something sparkling and red on your lips for tonight," Henri said to his wife now entering the living room, in that gracious French accent that had made her to fall in love with him.

The corners of her lips curved up, but her eyes betrayed her. "Will do."

She expected nothing less. Henri loved it when she wore a red lipstick. Well, more so that he loved the attention she garnered from his associates.

The only red thing she was allowed to own during their 20-year-long marriage was her lipstick.

Nicole discreetly wiped her clammy palms against her crisp baby pink cotton sundress that was a little snug on her figure. She tucked a loose strand of her blond hair behind her ear, just how Henri liked it. She couldn't wait for him to leave for work.

A cool breeze, thick with the scent of frangipani and the distant tang of salt, stirred gently, rustling the vibrant bougainvillea that cascaded over the veranda's railing. From the outside, the De Marigny residence stood as a testament to colonial elegance. A wide terrace wrapped around the house, furnished with cane outdoor chairs and pristine white seat covers that gleamed even in the dim light of dusk. Guests often gathered here during soirées sipping champagne and marvelling at the view of the sprawling gardens below.

As she watched Henri's eyes scan the headlines, she searched for the man she had met in London twenty years ago. The man who walked into the restaurant that day and took her breath away was not the man sitting across from her in a dark suit that was a touch too formal for the tropical climate. Every few sips from his steaming cup of coffee were punctuated by a disapproving glance at the newspaper he held unfolded in front of him.

Suddenly, Henri's eyes narrowed and his lips curled back in an ugly glare.

"Mareva!"

Nicole's palm squeezed into tight fists on her lap. She hated it when he yelled at Mareva, but that was often the case when he was in this ill mood. *Poor Mareva.*

The older lady shuffled out onto the veranda once again and stopped a few feet away from Henri with her eyes downcast and hands clasped behind her broad back. Everyone knew not to test Henri, especially when he was so irritable.

"Oui, Monsieur."

Henri snapped his fingers in Nicole's direction. "Make sure she looks perfect tonight."

"Oui, Monsieur."

"Remember, this dinner is for 24 people… don't make me repeat myself."

"Oui, Monsieur."

With that, Henri pushed himself to his feet and grabbed his briefcase. He didn't bother announcing his departure like a husband would to a wife. He always went off once he got the last word in.

Nicole held her breath as the echo of his footsteps became faint. She remained frozen in her seat until the front door was banged shut. After what felt like forever, and she was certain he had left, she slumped in her seat, finally feeling like she could breathe again, knowing she'd only see him again at nighttime. That might seem like a long time for another woman who had a happy home and a loving husband, however, Nicole was not that woman. If anything, nighttime was way too early.

She cherished the times when Henri would go on his business trips to locations he wouldn't disclose. She didn't mind because that meant she had the house all to herself — to do whatever she wanted, go wherever she wanted, and most importantly, wear whatever she wanted.

Lately, Henri had become more particular about her looks, and it was what hurt the most. Through the years, he always found something to complain about. At first, he would criticise her taste in fashion. He would often say, '*I know you grew up with nothing, but that does not mean you shouldn't know how to act. You're a wealthy woman now, act like it*', or '*That wouldn't look out of place back in your old neighbourhood*'. His words, laced with condescension, made her feel small and unworthy of her new status.

Over the years, his jabs became more personal, more pointed. When she had Lou, her body slightly changed, as a result of pregnancy, and that's when the subtle digs became outright criticism. Her smile, which he once deemed charming, was now too wide for a lady. He also had an issue with the way she walked, which he now deemed unbecoming. Even her voice was now met with a scathing, 'Can you quiet down a bit?'

His hurtful comments used to get to her, but now, they only caused slight discomfort. At forty, she would be kidding herself if she couldn't admit she was getting older. She was no longer the young woman Henri had married twenty years ago. She was still a beauty, but Henri was uncomfortable with the slight changes incurred by age. He hated the subtle silver in her hair, the little lines, and the tiny wrinkles that were only visible when she smiled.

Henri wasn't the spiciest in the bunch either, but he would rather fixate on all her flaws than his own. He didn't mind that he was getting older but how dare she age? The hypocrisy was laughable. Here he was, a man pushing fifty-five, with a thickening waistline and a receding hairline that he stubbornly refused to acknowledge. Yet, the audacity for her to age? Unthinkable!

"Madame would like a cup of tea?" Mareva's gentle voice cut through Nicole's increasing resentment. She looked up, surprised to see the maid standing expectantly by the doorway.

"Oh, Mareva," Nicole said, a touch flustered. "What were you saying?"

Mareva smiled, a kind crease appearing around her own eyes. "Can I get you anything, Madame?" She approached Nicole, concern etched on her face.

"Thank you, Mareva. No, I'm alright. Is he…?" Her voice trailed off.

Mareva, with her keen eyes that missed nothing, simply nodded and whispered "I saw him leave, Madame."

The kitchen window offered a direct view of the driveway, and Mareva always knew when Monsieur Henri had departed and when he returned.

"Good." Nicole slumped back in the chair with a deep exhale, the tension visibly draining from her shoulders. Her back hurting from holding a perfect posture for so long. "Now I can go back to my book and then I will phone my Mam" she thought.

Mareva went back to her duties, following Monsieur Henri's orders. When Henri gives orders, they are always followed. His absence was the only time there was peace in the grand but suffocating De Marigny household.

With her husband gone, Nicole followed Mareva to the living room. Inside, the house exuded wealth and tradition. The large kitchen gleamed with polished marble countertops and state-of-the-art appliances, though it rarely saw use beyond Mareva's tireless efforts. On the sideboard in the formal dining room, sat framed the photo of Henri's father, the founder of the empire.

Nicole sat on the brown leather chaise lounge opposite Mareva. The cream linen curtains had been pulled back, allowing natural light to streak into the room.

Mareva started ironing, and Nicole flipped open her novel. It wasn't surprising to see the maid and Madame in such a friendly position, although this was never the case when Henri was present because he always thought the maid was beneath their status and should be treated as such. But Nicole had become close to Mareva over the years. There was just something special about the elderly Creole woman who had served the De Marigny family for decades.

Whenever Henri would travel on one of his business trips, it was always her and Mareva at home. Even when Pierre and Lou were back home on holiday, they never spoke more than two words to her, so she still only had Mareva for company. They became quite used to each other's presence.

Now she just wished she could go to Port Louis for some shopping, but she had forgotten to ask Henri for permission to use the car. Yes, she had to ask for permission before she could do anything. Henri was controlling, and he would flip if she did anything without consulting him first.

That was the biggest change in her life that needed the most adjustment. It had taken a while for her to concede to the fact that she needed to ask Henri before she could do anything. Growing up, she never had to do that. Her parents had raised her like a bird, allowing her to fly and make her own decisions while being a solid rock behind her whenever she failed.

One would think if you lived a life of splendor and wealth as she did here in exotic Mauritius, you wouldn't think about the less glittery town of Middlesbrough. And why anyone would chose the cold and windy winters of the North East of England, when you can be bare feet on a hot beach all year round. But the truth was that no day went by that Nicole didn't think about home. Growing up was the happiest time of her life. They had all that they needed, and everyone was friendly to each other.

The vastness of the villa mocked her. It was perched atop a hill overlooking the beach. Sure, the view from her window was breathtaking. Le Morne was a majestic silhouette against the turquoise canvas of the ocean. She always felt small in the large rooms that were filled with imported furniture, unlike the rickety chairs they had back home, and mahogany and cane ceiling fans that whirred all day, relieving them from the heat and humidity of the Mauritian summer.

Her entire house back in Middlesbrough could fit in this room, a thought that brought a wry smile to her lips, quickly replaced by a sigh. There, she was Nicole, a free soul. Here, she was Madame De Marigny, a shiny ornament expected to live up to a name that felt increasingly foreign.

Despite all these luxuries, Nicole would choose Middlesbrough over and over again because at least there, she was happy. Sighing, she picked up her book again and forced herself to concentrate. The day was still long.

Later that evening, Nicole joined Mareva in the kitchen. Mareva was just adding the finishing touches to the dinner. Just then, Nicole felt a rush of adrenaline through her body.

"I didn't realise I had two maids," He growled behind them.

"Henri!" Nicole stuttered.

Neither Nicole nor Mareva knew Henri had arrived until his words snapped. They whirled around, wariness etched on their faces. The plate slipped from Nicole's hands and clattered to the floor.

"Good evening, Monsieur," Mareva greeted, quickly recovering from the shock. As tall as Henri was, he had a disconcerting way of sneaking up on people undetected.

He ignored Mareva and fixed his glare on Nicole. "Would you also like to scrub the floors and wash my car?"

"I—I". Nicole stammered, her mind racing for an explanation. "She was just showing me how to make a Crème Brûlée."

"Why?" Henri stood stoic in the center of the kitchen, his long fingers wrapped possessively around his briefcase handle. He loomed over them menacingly and Nicole couldn't help but wonder if he would make a scene before all his guests arrived.

"I don't need you to cook", he snapped. "If there's anything you should be learning, it's how to look more up to the standard of De Marigny which, if you haven't forgotten, is the name you carry!"

Nicole draw back, stung by his words. She had become immune to his abusive jabs over time, but sometimes, his insults still managed to pierce through the wall she had built around her heart.

"I'm sorry, Mareva," she gestured apologetically to the broken plate on the floor.

"It's not a problem, Madame," Mareva replied gently.

As Nicole walked past Henri, she heard him snap to Mareva, "Is everything ready for dinner?"

Nicole walked up the grand staircase to the master bedroom, her heart still pounding from the confrontation in the kitchen. She paused at the door, taking a deep breath before walking in.

Mareva had laid out an elegant dress on the king-sized bed. It was a flowing sundress in a color that resembled the fiery Mauritian sunset – a cascade of orange and pink shades.

Her legs were without a doubt, her best feature. She smiled, knowing Mareva did this on purpose to boost her confidence. She got dressed.

On the vanity was her red signature lipstick, just as Henri had ordered.

The door swung open, revealing Henri. He scanned her with a critical eye that lingered a beat too long on the exposed skin at her shoulders.

"Turn around", he commanded.

Nicole obeyed, slowly spinning so he could inspect her from all angles. He scrutinised her for a moment, his expression unreadable.

"It will do," he finally conceded, though his approval lacked conviction.

She glanced at herself in the mirror. This was her role, the beautiful, compliant wife. Tonight, as she had done for many years, she would play her role well. Henri was not the forgiving type, so she couldn't afford to be anything less than the perfect hostess. She took a deep breath and slipped her arm through his before walking out of the room.

The dining area was already bustling with activity when they descended. The long table was set with fine China, crystal glasses, and silverware, all shining under the soft light of the chandeliers.

Champagne flowed freely, filling the air with the sound of popping corks and bubbling laughter. Mareva had done a splendid job as always.

A blend of French cuisine with subtle local flavours made the house smell delicious.

The guests, who were a mix of socialites and business associates, mingled in animated conversation. Some were perched on plush velvet, blue chairs, and their laughter echoing off the high ceilings. Others stood in smaller groups with champagne flutes raised in a toast.

As soon as they reached the landing, Henri was whisked away by some of his friends to discuss business. Some of these "friends" happened to be young women. A hush fell over the room momentarily, then the chatter resumed now laced with curious glances in her direction. She plastered on a smile, her eyes searching for a familiar face.

Nicole moved through the room, exchanging polite smiles and greetings. She was used to seeing Henri close to other women at these gatherings. A wave of sadness washed over her, seeing her husband's arm draped over those young women in a way he no longer touched her.

Soon, it was time for dinner and they all took their places around the table. Aromas of lime, dill, goat cheese and honey delighted eyes and palates.

She glanced at Henri, who was deep in conversation with a young woman seated next to him.

Sensing her withdrawal, Henri leaned in and whispered, "Smile, darling."

Nicole nodded, forcing the smile back onto her face. To onlookers, they were two lovers sharing a tender moment, but that was the furthest thing from the truth.

Once he was satisfied, Henri returned to his conversation with the woman beside him. On cue, Henri placed a possessive hand on Nicole's thigh.

He always had a way of reassuring her, a way of making her believe everything was alright. Although their marriage was not perfect, she knew he loved her. At least, that's what she wanted to believe.

From where she was seated, Nicole could see the large eggshell painted kitchen and the flushed face of the busy maid, juggling between ovens and pans, drying her hand on her apron. Nicole suddenly felt overwhelmed by a feeling of nostalgia. That simple gesture was something her own mother did so often.

Tears were welling up. Nicole cleared her throat and dabbed her eyes.

No one noticed.

Chapter 2

"Ladies draped themselves in shawls of superiority, whilst men draw on their cigars blinded by the smoke of their arrogance."

"Henri?"

Nicole peeked into her husband's room the next morning. The air was embedded by the musky scent of his cologne. Henri stood before the mirror, meticulously adjusting his gold cufflinks. He paired his navy blue suit with a light blue shirt and shiny black shoes.

As he turned, the familiar coldness in his eyes threatened to send a shiver down Nicole's spine, but she held her ground instead of shrinking like she always did. Even though there was every reason to be wary of him, he was still her husband. The room was warm, and the gentle noise of the ceiling fan kept a steady tempo.

"What is it Nicole?" he grumbled as he walked towards the door. "You can see I'm in a hurry, and I haven't had my breakfast."

Despite the morning sun streaming through the shutters, the room felt suffocating. He brushed past her. Nicole followed close behind, her heels clicking softly against the tiled floor.

"I was just wondering about Pierre and Lou," she started, taking the stairs with him. "I've been trying to reach them, but to no avail. Have you heard from them?"

She knew he had. A knot of worry tightened in her stomach. This wasn't unusual, but a nagging fear troubled her.

Henri derisory gaze swept over her "So, you haven't heard from your own children? You have nothing to do all day, yet you fail at being a good wife. How can you *also* fail at being a mother?"

"I have *always* been their mother!" the words tumbled out before she could stop them. "I've been there for them more than you ever have!"

She hated it when he questioned her ability to care for their children. This was another facet of her life that caused her great pain.

Ignoring her outburst, Henri turned to her. "Well, while you were unable to connect to your kids, they called me to let me know they'll be back home next week."

It hurt Nicole so much that her kids had chosen to talk to their father instead of her. Since they became teenagers, they had drawn away from her and closer to their father for obvious reasons. He wasn't always available, but his money was. He was able to get them whatever they wanted, whenever they wanted it, and they took full advantage of that. It was unfair because her kids were the only thing she had, and Henri had succeeded in monopolizing their affection.

"Anything else?" He raised an eyebrow, a mocking smile playing on his lips.

"Can I take the car out today? I need to go see Lizzy." She braced herself for a refusal. Instead, he nodded once.

"Fine. But I need you to be back by five," he added and turned to walk into the dining room where Mareva already had his breakfast waiting.

The aroma of freshly brewed coffee and warm buttery croissants promised a far more pleasant experience than the tense exchange they had just had, but she was not hungry anymore. Still, Henri expected her to be a "lady" and show up for breakfast regardless of how she felt.

Shaking off her frustration, she straightened her back and forced a faint smile on her face before walking into the dining room. Mareva stood ready with steaming tea and coffee, a plate of pastries and freshly made fruit juices.

"Good morning, Madame," she greeted Nicole with a gentle smile.

"Good morning, Mareva," Nicole responded, her voice softer than it had been with Henri.

Nicole remembered the time when Mareva would barely acknowledge her. Back then, a gulf of unspoken animosity had separated them. Mareva had placed Nicole on a pedestal, a position that felt isolating and lonely. Thankfully, things had shifted over time. With Henri being absent most days, a sweet friendship had blossomed between the two women.

The deafening silence around the breakfast table was finally over. Henri had left and headed to his car.

"Are you going out Madame?" Mareva asked, her look flitting to the casual dress Nicole wore instead of her usual elegant attire.

"I'm going to Floreal."

"Ah, to Madame Lizzy?"

"Yes."

Lizzy was her closest friend, and right now, she wanted nothing more than to hear Lizzy's comforting words before she lost her mind. She said goodbye to Mareva and walked out the door. As she walked towards the garage, she heard the soft sounds of the ocean below and allowed it to take the pain away. The sleek, spotless, white convertible was sitting prettily in the garage.

With a hurried wave to Mareva, Nicole drove out of the garage and sped off the villa grounds. She could only truly breathe once her home was no longer in sight. Driving up to the hills with the breeze in her hair was the closest thing she had to freedom.

In a few minutes, Nicole was starting to feel the effect of the drive. Henri, her kids' behaviour, and her hurt—all fell away as she drove through the beautiful rows of red and green baobab trees. Soon, the vibrant chaos of the market of Quatre Bornes filled her field of vision. Stalls lined the narrow streets, overflowing with bright fabrics, piles of fresh fruits and vegetables, vibrant spices and fresh fish displayed on beds of ice. Vendors called out to passersby with enthusiasm. The air was thick with the aroma of local stews simmering in large pots, blending with the scent of rougaille— a typical Creole rich and spiced dish. Shouts and laughter in a medley of English, French, Creole and Tamil completed the charm.

Nicole slowed down to watch .The sight of happy youth brought a bittersweet smile to her face. It reminded her of her own childhood, the carefree days spent running around Middlesbrough with her friends. Oh, what she would give to be young and naïve again.

The sweltering heat of the coast gave way to a more pleasant warmth as she approached Vacoas on her climb toward Floreal. She hadn't seen Lizzy in a month, and she had a lot to talk to her friend about.

Lizzy's house was an hour away from Nicole's, and it felt like a different world altogether. Lizzy had once been a teacher in London, but she had spent many years teaching in Mauritius since relocating. Having lived in Mauritius for more years than Nicole, Lizzy spoke French fluently and had seamlessly integrated into the island's culture. She was the only friend Nicole had in Mauritius.

She finally turned into a long driveway .Floreal was nestled in the hills of Mauritius with a climate similar to a tropical greenhouse—warm, humid, and enveloped in lush greenery.

Unlike the imposing grandeur of her own villa, Lizzy's home had a welcoming warmth that Nicole wished she could bask in every day.

Even before she reached the mahogany inlaid door, it flew open and Lizzy appeared. Lizzy and Nicole were quite a contrasting pair. Lizzy was as brunette as Nicole was a blonde, tall where Nicole was shorter, and was such a lively character.

"Lizzy!" Nicole's voice tinged with relief and excitement.

"Nicole!" Lizzy's arms were already outstretched, her smile warm and welcoming. "It's been too long."

Nicole hugged her friend tightly. "I know. I've missed you so much."

"Come in, come in," Lizzy urged, leading her inside. "We have a lot to catch up."

As they walked into Lizzy's home, Nicole felt the weight of her worries lift, even if just for a moment. Here, in the company of her dear friend, she found a piece of the freedom and happiness she so desperately missed.

Nicole looked across the living room as she settled on the sofa next to her friend. It wasn't as grand or as opulent as her own but it somehow looked better. It was obvious that people truly lived in the house and had made good memories in it.

"How's Chris?" Nicole asked as Lizzy handed her a glass of freshly squeezed grapefruit juice.

Chris, Lizzy's husband, was a constant source of amusement and stability for them both. Judging by how quiet the house was, Nicole concluded he was still at work. This was good. Having the whole house to themselves mean she could freely pour her heart out to her friend.

They had three kids, all boys, who were in college at La Bourdonnais. The same college Pierre and Lou attended. So, whenever Chris was away, Lizzy was alone in their home. Nicole couldn't imagine how much worse life would have been if she had to spend her days alone in the villa. Thankfully, she had Mareva.

Nicole shook her head. "I don't know how you do it. I'd go crazy being in that house all by myself."

"I manage," Lizzy answered with a knowing smile. "Thankfully, Chris tries to come back as early as possible. What about you? How is Henri?"

Nicole shrugged her shoulders. "He's fine, I guess. I never know."

"That bad?"

"He's getting worse," Nicole answered honestly.

Lizzy's brows shot up. "Really?"

"Maybe I need to stop lying to myself. Maybe I need to do something."

"What you *need* to do is think about Pierre and Lou. Your kids need both of you."

This wasn't new. Nicole had thought through everything already. In fact, the only reason she had stayed this long was because of how much she loved her family. Even though her husband treated her the way he did, she loved him, and she loved their children.

Tears prickled at the corner of her eyes. "I don't think my kids want me in their lives anymore. I can feel them pulling away from me and I don't know how to stop it."

"Oh Nicole," Lizzy said softly, "I'm sure they love you very much."

"I know," Nicole sighed. "But they would rather be with their father than with me. Henri does a lot of things for them, I don't."

"Come on." Lizzy nudged her playfully. "Pierre is nineteen, and Lou is almost seventeen. I'm sure they know better than that."

Nicole laughed bitterly. "Then explain why they never call me, but they're always communicating with their Dad."

Although she was getting upset, Nicole held back her tears. "So, what's the whole point? They're the reason I'm holding back, but if they don't want me…"

Lizzy narrowed her eyes. "What are you saying, Nicole?"

"I'm tired, Lizzy, I'm not happy with Henri. I know I might sound ungrateful, but I'm not happy. I'm just not."

"Just calm down, Nicole. Your kids love you. They're teenagers, after all. Of course, they want all these expensive things, but I'm sure they know your love is worth more than all these together."

As usual, her friend knew all the right things to say to make her happy. They talked for hours, sharing stories and catching up on each other's lives. Nicole found comfort in Lizzy's company, appreciating her friend's understanding and support. Later on, they moved to the garden, sitting under the shade of a large palm tree. Lizzy brought out a jug of iced tea, and they sipped their drinks, enjoying the peaceful surroundings.

"I better get going," Nicole said, setting her glass on the table. "Henri will kill me if I'm late."

"Oh please. He probably just wants his wife all to himself," Lizzy giggled.

If only she knew how wrong she was.

"It's going to be okay," Lizzy continued. "Trust me, that man loves you. Your kids love you. And I need my friend, so don't go anywhere."

~~~

As Nicole pulled into the driveway, a sense of calm settled over her. Lizzy was right. Her children loved her. The memory of little Pierre and Lou, clinging to her legs and demanding bedtime stories, brought a smile to her face.

The sound of laughter and chatter filtered through the open windows as she approached the main door.

Nicole opened the door, stepping into a scene of lively chaos. Three of the De Marignys' closest families – the Moreaux, the Gauthiers, and the Duvals – were stretched out on the sofas, each holding a glass of gin and tonic. Henri was nowhere to be seen.

As she entered, the room fell silent. All eyes turned towards her, and the previously cheerful atmosphere receded slightly. The three couples, all impeccably dressed, rose respectfully to their feet. Nicole swallowed her shock and wore a smile on her face as she greeted them one by one.

"Oh, it's so nice to see you," she said, her voice strained but polite. "It's so wonderful to see you all."

Bernard Moreau, the only man in their circle as tall as Henri, held her shoulders and smiled down at her. "Bonjour, ma belle. You look radiant tonight."

"Merci, Bernard," Nicole replied, before turning to the others.

"I hope you're all comfortable?"

A chorus of affirmations filled the room. "Very much, Nicole," replied Isabelle Gauthier.

Nicole nodded. "I'm going to freshen up. I'll be with you all in a moment."

Eyebrows were raised. Suffused giggled were heard.

With a forced lightness in her step, Nicole took the stairs, her smile fading as quickly as it had appeared. A wave of hot, suffocating anger washed over her.

This little gathering was clearly a blatant snub. Henri hadn't bothered to mention it, leaving her completely unprepared and, worse, feeling like an outsider in her own home. She felt disrespected, more so because she now had to play the role of the perfect, sweet host.

Reaching the landing, she walked down the hallway towards Henri's room.

She opened the door without knocking. This was something she had never done before, but she was fuming this time.

Henri, startled by the intrusion, spun around from the mirror, his face hardening into an angry stare. "Nicole!" he snapped. "How dare you barge in this way?"

"There are guests downstairs!" she hissed, barely containing her irritation. "Why wasn't I informed about this?"

Henri rolled his eyes. "I told you to be back before five. Your fault!"

"Henri," her voice trembled, "why you didn't say? Was it so much to ask?"

"Enough! This is my house, Nicole. Don't you ever forget that! I can do whatever I like. If you don't like it, you can go back to your poor little town and to your beggar of a mother."

He pushed past her and disappeared down the stairs. Tears welled up in her eyes, but she blinked them back fiercely. She couldn't afford to have swollen eyes in front of their guests. Taking a deep breath, she walked to the vanity. After a quick retouch of her makeup and changing into a more high-end dress, she hurried to join their guests downstairs.

Dinner was served on the large veranda of the villa that offered a panoramic view of the tropical garden and the serene beach of Tamarin. The smell of frangipane flowers was inebriating—a combination of almond and vanilla. It was an exotic fragrance, warm and inviting.

When she arrived on the veranda, she was taken aback by how quickly the guests had multiplied. As she moved through the crowd, her eyes fell upon a group of strikingly attractive women. These ladies were not only effortlessly beautiful but also had an air of confident sophistication. Clearly, they came from wealthy backgrounds.

She made her way to their oval shaped swimming pool. It buzzed with girls giggling and splashing each other, their voices carrying across the plantation. Nicole missed the days when the pool echoed with her children's laughter instead. Pierre and Lou used to race each other, their wet footprints trailing through the house.

Nicole's heart sank as she noticed her husband, Henri, engaging with those young ladies in a manner that seemed overly familiar.

Henri, in his element, chatted animatedly with the women, caressing a hand here, brushing a shoulder there, and sometimes just resting his hand on the small of a woman's back.

Trying to assert her presence, Nicole placed her hand on Henri's arm, hoping to re-establish her role as his wife. However, Henri, with a practised ease, gently removed her hand and continued his conversation with one of the single ladies. Her attempts to catch his eye or join in the conversation were met also with polite but dismissive responses.

Although all the guests were having a good time, it felt as they were all watching her embarrassing attempts unfold and laugh about it. Of course, this was all in her head. Most probably no one was paying attention to her.

As the dinner progressed, the air buzzed with chatter, a blend of French and English punctuated by bursts of laughter. Champagne flowed. Nicole, finding herself increasingly isolated sought a moment alone with Henri. She caught him by the veranda railing, overlooking the garden, and seized the opportunity to confront him, keeping her voice as low as possible.

"Henri, what's going on here? Why are you so friendly with these women?"

Henri glanced at her, a slight frown creasing his brow. "You're imagining things again. I'm simply being a good host. It's only natural to engage with the guests, which you should be doing instead of policing me."

"But—"

"But nothing. I'm just being nice to my guests. That's all. Don't ruin the evening with your stupid jealousy."

With that, he smiled and turned back to his guests, leaving Nicole standing alone. At this point, she didn't know why she bothered. The same thing happened at every dinner party they hosted, and even at other occasions where they were guests.

She brushed her husband's behaviour off and decided to enjoy the evening. Soon, she found herself laughing and engaging in conversations. Nicole had a talent for making others feel at ease, even when she, herself, was not. For a few hours, she allowed herself to forget her crumbling marriage and simply enjoy the evening.

Finally, as the guests began to leave, Mareva was already clearing the table, and Nicole felt gratitude for her silent support. She knew that whatever happened, she could always count on Mareva. No one ever complimented Mareva for her exquisite banquets. Nicole, however, always took a moment to thank Mareva privately, knowing how much it meant to her.

Chapter 3

"Welcome To the Republic of Mauritius". Nicole smiled, reading the sign.

Finally, she could be with the love of her life. Although she was only 20, Henri de Marigny was the man of her dreams, and she knew it from the day they met. He was everything any woman would ever want in a man—handsome, wealthy, a complete gentleman.

Henri walked up to her in his signature navy suit with the most handsome smile on his face. His eyes traveled from hers down to her neck, and suddenly, the corners of his lips turned downward.

"What is this?" he asked with disdain.

Her smile faltered as she loosened her scarf and held it up for him to see. "Oh, it's my scarf!"

The red and white scarf of her beloved football club was her pride and joy as the sole reminder of her home. Even now, standing in front of her husband, she could imagine the electric atmosphere of match day as everyone shuffled to the Riverside Stadium with swarms of other fans, a sea of red and white.

Her father used to take her and her friends to watch Middlesbrough FC in action. Sometimes, they would watch the boys play football in the streets, the smoke from the steel furnaces billowing in the background. There is something inexplicably comforting in the miserable greyness of Middlesbrough...

The sound of chants and songs resonated through the town, creating a powerful celebration of their shared passion. The smell of pies and burgers wafted from food stalls, mixed with the crisp, cool air of a typical Middlesbrough autumnal afternoon.

Henri's cold voice cut through her beautiful memory. "Do you think it's appropriate to wear that here?"

Nicole felt a sharp pain in her chest. "It's just a scarf, Henri," she replied, trying to keep her voice steady. "It reminds me of home."

"This is your home now," he said, gesturing around as if to encompass the entire island. "And that," he pointed to the scarf, "doesn't belong here."

Before she could react, he grabbed the scarf and tossed it in a nearby bin. When he walked back to her, he snapped his fingers for the chauffeur she hadn't noticed earlier, and the man rushed to take her luggage from her.

Henri adjusted his tie as he stared her down. "The only red thing you're allowed to have is your lipstick."

He spun around and took off towards the parking lot, undoubtedly expecting her to follow. She hurried behind him, wondering if this truly was the charming man she'd met back at the restaurant in London.

As they left the terminal and headed towards their car, Nicole couldn't shake the feeling of loss. Mauritius was beautiful, a paradise in many ways, but it wasn't Middlesbrough. In that moment, she realised how much she missed the simple joy of the familiar sights and sounds of her hometown.

"Madame?"

A gentle hand shook Nicole's shoulder.

"Madame?"

Nicole's eyes peeled open. "Mareva?"

"Yes, Madame, you fell asleep," Mareva said softly. "Monsieur Henri is back."

"Oh no, I didn't realise I had fallen asleep. Thank you, Mare—"

The older woman had already hurried off with a tray in her hand before Nicole could finish her sentence.

Disappointment washed over Nicole as she took in her surroundings. Indeed, she had fallen asleep while attempting to read a book. She instantly wished the dream she had just had of her hometown was her reality again. Had she been arriving at the airport now, knowing what she knew, she would have turned around and caught the next plane back to England.

How blind and naïve she had been all those years ago to not see the judgment in his eyes. Henri was arrogant, condescending, and controlling, among other things. Her 20-year-old self had perceived this as charm. Now, she knew better.

Suddenly, a loud growl and a crash interrupted her thoughts. Nicole quickly got out of bed and rushed downstairs to find Henri standing over Mareva, who was kneeling over a spilled tray, picking up the pieces of the broken mug. Henri was holding his suitcase tightly, glaring at Mareva.

"What happened?" Nicole asked, rushing to help Mareva.

"Go get ready," he snapped at Nicole. "Pierre and Lou will be landing at Sir Seewoosagur Ramgoolam in an hour."

Nicole frowned. "What? They're arriving in an hour? You told me they'd be here next week."

"They moved it up. Is there a problem?"

When they were younger, Pierre and Lou always wanted to be near her. As they grew older, their affection turned towards money, of which their ever-absent father had in abundance.

At some point, Nicole stopped caring about her husband's long and shady business trips and focused more on raising her children. Sadly, the more Henri showered their kids with money and gifts, the less they cared about her. Now they were teenagers who had needs she couldn't provide. Still, they were the only reason she was still in Mauritius, fighting to make her marriage work.

Nicole swallowed her frustration. "What number can I reach them on?" she asked, trying to keep her tone neutral. There were many issues she wanted to address, but now wasn't the time. Her priority was seeing her children.

"I'll forward it to you," Henri said, throwing a final glare at Mareva before storming out. The tension in the room dissipated the moment he left, and Nicole and Mareva exchanged relieved glances.

"It's not your fault, Mareva," Nicole said gently, helping her clean up. "He has no right to treat you like that."

Mareva sighed. "Désolé Madame. I just panicked."

"Don't apologise," Nicole insisted. "Let's just get ready for the kids. Can you please help me to prepare their rooms and if you could make their preferred clafoutis. Thank you Mareva"

An hour later, Nicole stood at the airport terminal, eagerly awaiting her children's arrival. The anticipation of seeing Pierre and Lou after so long made her momentarily forget her earlier tensions. As she spotted them among the crowd, her heart swelled with joy.

"Pierre! Lou!" she called out, waving frantically. They looked so grown-up, with Pierre's tall, slim build and Lou's beauty mirroring her own.

"Pierre! Lou!" she called again, louder this time. They finally noticed her and made their way over. Nicole enveloped them in a tight hug, laughing with delight.

"Oh, how good to see you!" she exclaimed.

"You too, Mam," they mumbled, though Pierre seemed distracted, already checking his phone.

Lou peered around Nicole. "Et Papa? I thought he was picking us up."

"He's at work, chérie," Nicole replied as she led them through the busy terminal, towards the car. Once they settled in the car, she tried to engage them. "So, how are you? How's your lives in Paris? How's school? Tell me everything."

Pierre, still engrossed in his phone, sighed. "Mam, it's school. How do you think we are?"

"Don't be rude," Lou scolded him sharply.

"Lou?"

"Mam, school was exhausting. I'm happy to be back home."

Nicole smiled back, though Pierre's lack of interest bothered her more than she was letting on. "So, Lou, what do—?"

"Mam, can you drop us off at the plantation's offices?" Pierre interrupted.

Nicole's eyes widened. "At your dad's office? But why? He'll be home tonight."

She glanced in the rearview mirror in time to see Pierre roll his eyes. He had been so unpleasant since he arrived and she couldn't help but wonder why.

"Yes, Mam, I need to see him too," Lou added.

Nicole pursed her lips. "What's so urgent? I thought we could spend some time together this afternoon."

Lou leaned forward, "I need a new phone. This one is so old, and all my friends are laughing at it. I'm sure Dad will get me a new one."

Pierre looked up. "And I want a motorbike."

Nicole was taken aback. "Pierre, you already have a new car. Your dad got it for you last year."

"That was last year," Pierre retorted, frowning.

"It cost your father a lot of money," Nicole argued. "And now you want a motorbike?"

"You didn't argue when Lou mentioned a new phone," Pierre shot back.

"You can't seriously compare a phone to a motorbike, can you? I don't think Lou needs a new phone; this one is barely six months old."

Lou suddenly shot her a look. "Mam!"

"Please Lou don't raise your voice at me," Nicole said. She sighed, turning her attention back to Pierre who was openly raging. "As I was saying, Lou's phone is not exactly cheap but it's not as expensive as a motorbike."

"Whatever, Mam," Pierre muttered, clearly dismissing her opinion. "Luckily, Dad doesn't need your permission to buy anything. It's his money, after all."

The comment cut deep, leaving Nicole speechless. They decided to ignore her and continued to discuss their plans in the backseat, confident in their father's willingness to indulge them, completely alienating Nicole.

Nicole veered off the road leading home and took the turn towards the plantation with a heavy heart. An endless queue of lorries overflowing with harvested sugarcane were disappearing behind them on the dusty track. She stopped just outside the Estate main offices. Pierre immediately got out of the car without a goodbye and walked towards the office. Lou leaned forward to press a kiss to her mother's cheek. "Merci, Maman," she said. "We will see you at home."

Her heart sank as she watched her children walk away. Pierre was getting more distant by the day, and although Lou wasn't all bad, there was really no difference. As she drove back home alone, she couldn't shake the feeling that she was losing her children, just as she had lost herself in this foreign land and unfulfilling marriage.

Chapter 4

"All that glitters is not gold."
-Shakespeare

~MAREVA~

The morning sun cast a beautiful golden glow through the grand dining room as Mareva moved with practiced grace, setting the breakfast table. The air was filled with every breakfast delicacy De Marigny children required.

Monsieur Henri had just left for work, and Madame Nicole and the kids would be up very soon. Breakfast in the house was usually light and simple, but with De Marigny children present, it required a lot more effort than usual. Pierre and Lou were hard to please, so Mareva had to pay close attention to how she baked the bread, scrambled the eggs, prepare the coffee, and so on.

Mareva was never granted a respite. Her days were punctuated by orders and chores.

The vastness of the household required her attendance well into the night.

As a woman of Creole descent, her skin was rich with the hues of the island sun, bearing the weight of her ancestors on her shoulders. Her ancestors had been brought to Mauritius as slaves and forced to toil in the sugarcane fields. Their spirits were broken and there had been bodies worn down by the intense labour. Yet, they were resilient and passed this strength down through the generations. It was this resilience that allowed Mareva to navigate the challenges of her role in the De Marigny household.

Her lips curved into a sad smile as she remembered that fateful day 20 years ago when a young Madame Nicole walked through the front door. Mareva instantly envied the younger woman who arrived in plain clothes that looked like they had been washed one too many times. The young Madame would soon become the epitome of beauty and grace once she was touched by the De Marigny wealth.

If she was completely honest with herself, she had resented her for being given the fairytale life so many maids dreamed of. Mareva would silently watch Madame Nicole try on the finest of clothes and adorn herself in the most expensive jewelry and perfumes, wishing she could experience such an opulent life too.

As the years passed, Mareva realised that she had the freedom her ancestry had lost. She wasn't wearing their rusty shackles. Nicole in the other hand, although free, was sadly trapped in golden chains.

Mareva shook her head, adjusted her apron over her blue blouse and walked back to the kitchen. Just as she passed the stairs, she heard a faint sniffle and froze, her ears perking up. She waited, and after a few seconds, the sniffle sounded again.

It was Madame Nicole, the sound coming from the master bedroom. Mareva hesitated, caught between duty and compassion. She didn't want to overstep her boundaries.

Madame Nicole's silent sniffles soon escalated into sobs and Mareva knew she couldn't just leave her alone in such distress. Mareva understood that sound. It was the cry of a woman who had everything, yet seemed to possess nothing.

With a deep breath, she made her way up the stairs and down the hallway toward the master bedroom. With a hesitant hand, she gently knocked on the door and then pushed it open.

The room was twice as large as Mareva's entire house. Madame Nicole lay curled up on the bed, her body trembling and her face buried in a pillow.

"Madame?" Mareva's voice was calm, as she walked up to the four-poster bed.

"Madame?" she called again, her voice soft, but Nicole only sobbed harder. Mareva stood at the foot of the bed, unsure whether it was appropriate to sit or pull her up. After a moment of indecision, she gently pulled Nicole into a sitting position. "It's okay, Madame. You're alright."

"Am I?" Nicole looked up, her face streaked with tears. "Am I?" she repeated, her voice shaky. "Or am I just kidding myself and pretending everything is fine when it isn't?"

"Madame..." Mareva's heart ached for her. She knew the answer, but the words felt inadequate. Instead, she took Nicole's hand, squeezing it gently.

She had witnessed the life Madame Nicole lived—a life that seemed luxurious on the surface but was filled with silent suffering. Her husband treated her with cold disrespect, and now even the children were beginning to mirror his behaviour.

Mareva had her own burdens too. Although slavery had long been abolished, the social and economic disparities were still very present, and Mareva knew this all too well. The best opportunity she had been given in life was to be a maid to a wealthy family. Similarly, the best her husband Baptiste could do was to be a chauffeur for the same household. She had accepted this as their fate.

"Mareva, I'm doing all I can for them," Nicole continued, her voice cracking. "I'm trying so hard, but because I don't buy them the latest phones or the latest cars, I'm useless."

"No—" Mareva tried to interject, but Nicole's sobs drowned her out. She felt a surge of compassion and decided it might be best to get Nicole out of the house, if only for a little while. Nicole enjoyed walking along the beach on quiet mornings like this, and Mareva thought the fresh air might help.

"Come on," Mareva prompted gently.

"Where are we going?"

"The weather is so nice this morning. A walk on the beach might do you good." Nicole nodded, not arguing. The beach wasn't far. They descended the Morcellement and walked together, passing the dazzling white salt farms.

The salt pans stretched out before them, shimmering under the rays of the morning sun. The women walked in silence.

As they walked, Nicole wrapped her arms around herself, sighing heavily. Mareva had intended this walk to calm Nicole, but she found the rushing blue waters soothing to her own soul as well. They stopped at the shore. On the other side, people lounged on chairs and swam in the sea.

Nicole sighed. "I don't want anyone to see me crying. They'll probably think I'm an ungrateful woman who has everything and still isn't happy."

"Pardon me if I'm being too forward, Madame, but how did you meet Monsieur Henri?" Mareva asked cautiously. There was a long pause, and Mareva feared she had crossed a boundary.

"When I was eighteen, I started working as a waitress in one of the big restaurants in London.

Henri was there for a conference, and that's where we met." Nicole smiled faintly, a hint of nostalgia in her eyes. Mareva sensed that, despite everything, Madame Nicole was still in love with her husband. It was too personal a question to ask outright, so instead, Mareva asked a different question.

"Was he different then?"

"He was the sweetest," Nicole said softly. "He was really sweet, and I fell madly in love. So much so that even after everything, I still love him now." She sighed, touching her golden necklace. "We flown to Cartier in Paris just to purchase my necklace. He used to hold the door open, buy me flowers and expensive jewelry... I felt like the luckiest girl in the world. I was desperate to leave the council house, so I was ecstatic when he proposed a few months later." Nicole shook her head. "I didn't realise I'd miss home so much, but when I came here, I realised it's better to have nothing and be happy than to have everything and be unhappy."

"I'm sorry," Mareva said, shaking her head.

"For what?" Nicole shrugged. "I chose this life."

They spent nearly an hour on the beach, talking about everything. Mareva learned more about Nicole's parents and her best friends back in Middlesbrough. She felt a deepening sadness for Madame Nicole, who seemed trapped. Her life wasn't as pretty as it was on the outside. It made Mareva appreciate her life with Baptiste more.

"I have to go back to make dinner," Mareva said with a quiet sigh. "Monsieur Henri will be back soon."

"Monsieur Henri," Nicole repeated with a shudder, causing Mareva to chuckle. "Come on then, let's go back."

"I'll need to stop briefly at my house first," Mareva said. "I have to give some instructions to my grandchildren for dinner."

"Oh, can I come with you? I'd love to finally meet them!"

Mareva hesitated, feeling a mix of concern and embarrassment. Her house in Tamarin was a tiny shack behind a noisy convenience store, the complete opposite of the opulence of the De Marigny villa. Still, Madame Nicole pleaded, so Mareva had no choice but to comply, and they set off on their way.

"It's not much," Mareva said as they approached the building. "But it's home."

"It's perfect," Nicole replied with a warm smile, surprising Mareva. She wondered what Madame Nicole saw in her modest home, especially after spending all her days in the grandeur of the villa. It made sense for Mareva to feel like her home was heaven because she had made precious memories with her husband and children, but it didn't make sense for a De Marigny to think there was anything perfect about her home.

They walked into the living room to find it nearly empty. Mareva lived here with her grandchildren when she wasn't at work. Her sons worked long hours, leaving their boys in her care. Despite the cramped quarters and lack of luxury, there was warmth in this little home; a warmth born of family bonds. After Nicole stepped inside for the first time, she noticed the mismatched furniture: two sofas... one that sagged and was covered with a hand-embroidered cloth, a small altar adorned with faded photographs of ancestors, and a table where meals were shared amidst stories told in Creole .It was humble but full of life, unlike the cold magnificence of her own home.

The house was smaller inside than it looked from the outside. However, the old sofas weren't the most embarrassing thing in the living room. Mareva and Baptiste had placed steel buckets in some corners of the living room to catch water droplets because the roof was leaky. Mareva felt a flush of embarrassment as Madame Nicole stared at one of the buckets.

"It's for catching water when it rains at monsoon time. The roof leaks," Mareva explained.

Nicole smiled, her eyes softening with understanding. "Back home, I had buckets like this in my room. I had to wake up at intervals to empty them, or else the house would flood."

They both laughed, breaking the tension. Just then, Mareva's boys walked into the living room.

"Bonzour Granmer'," they greeted their Grandmother in creole, kissing her on her cheeks. Mareva's heart swelled with pride as she introduced them.

"Boys, this is Madame Nicole. She's Monsieur Henri De Marigny's wife." Then she pointed to her grandsons. "Madame, these are Joseph and Claude. Their parents work all day at Le Paradis. My sons are both working in the hotel's kitchen and finish very late every night and I am happy to help them by keeping the boys with me.

The boys greeted Nicole respectfully. "Grandma only has good things to say about you," Joseph said. "You're welcome to our home."

"Oh merci. Such lovely boys".

Mareva smiled. She gave them instructions for dinner and then left with Madame Nicole.

"Your boys are wonderful," Nicole commented, with genuine adoration in her voice.

"Thank you, Madame." Mareva thought of Nicole's children, Pierre and Lou, and the sadness in Nicole's eyes whenever she spoke of them. It was a shame they had turned out that way. Mareva wished nothing but happiness for her Madame.

As they walked back to the villa, the gentle breeze suddenly picked up speed, becoming more violent every few minutes. The build-up of humidity over the afternoon had attracted dark, heavy clouds.

The two women walked more hurriedly than before to avoid the oncoming monsoon. Shame they could not avoid Monsieur Henri in a similar fashion. For the first time, they enjoyed each other's company without the fear of his sudden arrival.

Chapter 5

~ HENRI~

Henri De Marigny is a silver-haired, middle aged man with an austere look and piercing blue eyes. He carried himself with an air of self-importance and assertive stride. He thrived on routine. Every morning, he woke at the same time, brushed his teeth, showered, and dressed in one of his expensive suits. Breakfast was a thirty-minute affair, meticulously timed so he could be at work by eight a.m. This routine had been his unwavering practice for years. But today was different.

At seven a.m., Henri was already dressed and ready, but instead of heading downstairs for breakfast, he went straight to see Nicole.

He didn't regret marrying Nicole, as their marriage had given him Pierre and Lou. However, he sometimes wished he had married someone of his own social status. The first time he laid eyes on Nicole, he was blinded by her beauty, leading him to make dumb decisions he shouldn't have—like marrying her.

Nicole was a poor woman, and nothing was ever going to change that. No amount of money in the world would change her at heart. The only advantage she had going was that she was still beautiful, if not, he would have reconsidered about her presence in his house.

"Can we talk?" he asked, standing in the doorway of her room.

"Sure," Nicole replied, gesturing to the couch. "Sit down."

"No need for that; I'm running late for work," he said curtly. "I just need you to listen."

She nodded, a touch of apprehension in her eyes. "I'm listening."

"Nicole, I've told you countless times that when it comes to the kids, I should be the one making all the decisions. I don't think you're capable of making sound choices for their future."

Her eyes narrowed defensively. "Is this about yesterday?"

"Partly," he frowned. "It's about yesterday and all the other times."

"So just because they rushed to you, you don't think you should ask me what happened?"

"Is that necessary?" Henri huffed. "Pierre and Lou are teenagers. They know what they want and need."

"They are *my* kids too, Henri. Pierre and Lou are *also* my kids. And you know that all they do is talk on the phone and play games all day."

"They're on holiday Nicole!" Henri defended. "What's wrong with playing games and talking on the phone? The last time I saw their grades, they were doing just fine."

Nicole threw her arms up in the air. "That's the problem!" She huffed. "They can't have everything they want. It's an important lesson to teach them."

Henri raised a finger and she instantly fell silent. He was getting late, which was out of his character, but he couldn't resist making his point.

"I see there's a misunderstanding here", he said coldly. "Pierre and Lou are *De Marignys*," he said, pride swelling in his voice. "They're fortunate to be born into one of the wealthiest families, which is probably the only good thing you've done for them."

She gasped, but he ignored it and continued.

"Don't you *ever* mistake them for yourself, Nicole *Robinson*. That's where you're wrong."

Nicole's folded her lips to hide the trembling, but he had already seen her weakness on display.

"What are you saying, Henri?"

He took one step forward, fully cementing his presence in her room. "Just because you're their mother doesn't mean they should have a life as hard as yours."

"My life wasn't hard," Nicole's voice trembled. "Poor, but not hard. Money isn't everything."

Henri adjusted his tie. "Oh, but it is, my dear," Henri countered. "If not for my money, you wouldn't be here as the Madame of this villa. Even your father couldn't have ever dreamed of owning something of such magnificence while he was alive."

His words knocked the wind out of her. "Henri..."

"If not for my money," he continued raising his voice, "you would still be stuck in that gloomy town of yours back in England, looking stressed and washed up. But look at you now."

"Henri!"

"My kids are not *you*, Nicole. Get that into your head!"

He exhaled as though he had been carrying a heavy load on his shoulders, then took another step forward. "Don't you ever forget this one thing: Pierre and Lou are *De Marignys*, not Robinsons, and they will *never* taste a hard life like you."

He turned to leave and paused with his hand on the door handle. "Be ready by six. I'll come to pick you up. There's a dinner we need to attend."

With that, he disappeared from the room without offering any additional information. He hated having to explain himself to those beneath him. So, he never did.

Chapter 6

"Nicole, it's ridiculous! This is a blessing! You're leaving Middlesbrough for Mauritius, you silly girl. What is there to think about?"

Nicole remembered these words vividly. That was what Melanie said the day Nicole told her friends about Henri's proposal twenty years ago. They were coming from the stadium where Middlesbrough had won a home match. Henri had proposed the night before, and she was still mulling it over.

"You have to say yes", Jen added. *"Henri is so handsome and rich, and he buys you all these little gifts. What more do you want?"* Those words resounded even more compelling through the red bricks rows of terraced houses.

At the time, Nicole had wanted nothing more. Henri was her Prince Charming, wealthy and fascinating, showering her with gifts and attention.

When they arrived at Nicole's council house that evening, Henri was standing outside with a bouquet of roses and another box of jewelry, pleading for her to be his wife. She had said 'yes' without hesitation.

Soon after there she was, having just landed in Mauritius with only one hand luggage but a heart full of love .Their wedding day on the never ending white sandy beach was nothing less than a magical, perfect day. Now, 20 years later, she realised it was the worst mistake she had ever made.

Nicole paced the room, wondering how she had missed the signs. She let the tears flow freely down her cheeks. She wanted to call her Mam or Lizzy, but they were probably tired of listening to her complain about the same things over and over again. She sank onto the bed and held her head pitifully.

The sound of heavy downpour relentlessly beating against the windows mirrored the storm which had been raging within her heart for years. But she knew better than to let her emotions show for too long. Henri wouldn't tolerate it.

Taking a deep breath, Nicole wiped her tears and rose from the bed. She had to get ready for dinner. Henri expected her to be perfect, and she couldn't afford to get on his bad side. She walked to her wardrobe, opening the doors to reveal an array of dresses. Her eyes immediately landed on a sleek black statement dress that seemed to be calling out to her. The colour matched her mood.

The dress was made of soft, flowing silk that hugged her figure perfectly, flaring slightly at the hips before falling gracefully to her ankles. It had a high neckline, which contrasted with the daring open back that added a touch of sophistication and allure, just as Henri liked. The long, seductive slit on one side allowed for elegant movement as she walked.

Despite her sombre mood, Nicole reached for her makeup kit. She decided on a more natural look, which was what she preferred. Of course, the other women would judge her as they always did, but she had no energy for "*full glam*" tonight. Her hands hesitated as she picked up the red lipstick. For once, she wanted to wear a shade of her choosing, but ever obedient, she brought it to her lips and carefully applied it. She stared at her reflection in the mirror trying to recognise the woman she had become. These days, she found herself staring at her reflection more and more often. Whatever she was looking for, was not present behind the dead eyes that stared back at her.

She adjusted her dress and checked one last time in the mirror, smoothing her blonde hair and ensuring everything was in place. The monsoon's growing intensity only seemed to heighten her sense of isolation. Yet, she knew she had to face the evening with grace and poise, no matter how turbulent her emotions were.

Nicole straightened her posture, took a deep breath, and walked out of her room. It was always best to wait for Henri rather than have him wait for her. He hated waiting.

As she calmed herself and put on her practiced smile, the rain suddenly stopped, leaving behind the familiar uncomfortable humidity that Nicole had become accustomed to.

Henri picked her up at exactly six o'clock. She knew how punctual he was and made sure she was ready before he arrived. She had actually chosen this dress because it was one of Henri's favourite dresses.

Every time she wore it, he would hold her close all night. She desperately wanted to connect with her husband again.

This time, however, when she slipped into the car, Henri didn't even glance at her. "Good evening," she greeted. "How was work?"

"Fine. How are you?"

"Fine, thank you." There was nothing else to say. They had never really shared much in common.

Instead of worrying about the man next to her, Nicole decided to sit back and enjoy the view. Baptiste had taken the coastal road, a route that always offered a stunning view of the island's natural beauty. She didn't mind that she had seen these places before; they were still beautiful in her eyes.

The greenery of Mauritius framed the crystal clear waters of the Indian Ocean. Palm trees swayed gently in the breeze.

As they approached Grand Baie, the signs of tourism became more pronounced. Chic boutiques and upscale restaurants lined the streets, catering to the influx of visitors who came to experience the island's wonders. Soon, the vibrant nightlife, filled with bars and clubs would awaken. But even this lively scene couldn't lift Nicole's spirits. She felt like a spectator in her own life, watching the joy and excitement of others while she struggled with her own silent despair. This was the paradise many knew and dreamed of. This was the paradise that had become a living nightmare for her.

"Where are we going?" she asked when it dawned on her that they were now in Grand Baie.

"Le Royal Palm," Henri answered, typing away on his phone. He hadn't looked at her since she entered the car. She could easily have been replaced by someone else, and he wouldn't have noticed.

"Who's going to be there?" she asked.

He finally looked up, but his eyes didn't flare with admiration for how pretty she looked or how elegant her dress was, instead, they narrowed in irritation.

"What kind of question is that? Don't you know all the people we have dinner with? You talk like you've never been here before."

Nicole said nothing and just waited until they arrived at their destination. It wouldn't matter even if he told her who would be present because she didn't like most of his friends anyway. They were no different from Henri himself and they never truly accepted her. They always looked down on her and mocked her interests, with Henri egging them on. The only thing they appreciated about her was her beauty.

A few minutes later, Henri escorted Nicole into the Royal Palm, one of the most luxurious resorts in Mauritius. The facade of the building was a blend of colonial and contemporary architecture, painted in soft shades of beige and white, giving it a timeless, sophisticated look.

A uniformed attendant greeted them at the entrance and led them to the private terrace that overlooked the ocean. The place was beautifully decorated with lanterns illuminating their path heading to their table. The long table that was already occupied by Henri's friends.

When the couples noticed them approaching, they all stood up with smiles on their faces. Nicole thought the smiles were fake, but she smiled back politely. After exchanging pleasantries, she and Henri took their seats.

"We've been waiting for you," Bernard Moreau said. "What happened?"

"Sorry we're late," Henri said with the perfect smile he reserved for public appearances. "Nicole needed all the time in the world to get ready. You know how women are."

The others laughed, but Nicole didn't find it funny. "That seems fine," Bernard said. "I can see it paid off well. You look ravishing, Nicole."

The others murmured in agreement, and Nicole forced a smile. "Thank you."

When the waiters came over to take their orders, Henri snapped his fingers at a particularly attractive waitress. Nicole silently watched as her husband turned on his charm.

Although it was painfully obvious, she pulled the menu over her face, acting as though she couldn't see what was happening right beside her. And after five very long minutes of Henri stalling the waitress, their orders were finally taken. Henri's flirtations were no secret. At parties, he moved effortlessly between women, his charm oozing like honey. Nicole often caught whiffs of unfamiliar perfumes clinging to his shirts, subtle reminders of his late-night escapades. After returning home at late hours with lipstick marks on his suit, he always managed to convince her she was imagining things. "You're too sensitive," he'd say, brushing off her concerns with practiced ease.

The finest dinner was soon served, and the conversation turned to Henri's sugarcane business.

"So, Nicole," Gilles Arnault began, "what do you think about Henri's decision to build the best golf course on the island?"

The table fell silent, and the food turned sour in Nicole's mouth. She swallowed and looked up at the faces around her. "I..." she hesitated. No matter how much she tried, Henri never let her get involved in the business. She knew nothing about it, so she definitely had no idea Henri was looking to diversify.

After a few seconds of tense silence, Henri laughed. "She doesn't know anything about the business, Gilles."

"Why not?" Gilles Arnault frowned as if someone had just taken his favorite dessert from him.

Henri shrugged. "Nicole would rather bake with the maid than do any meaningful work."

As the table dissolved into laughter, Nicole felt her throat close up and heat rise up her face as she struggled to maintain a polite smile.

Trudi Meyers leaned forward, purposely revealing more of her plunging neckline. "I don't know how women choose kitchen work over business," she smirked. "But again, I understand that not everyone is as ambitious as me. Isn't that so?"

"Yes, darling," her husband Xavier replied, kissing her cheek. "Trudi runs the show in our business. It gives me time to relax and do other things because I know she's in charge."

"Oh, I wish," Henri snorted, taking a sip of his wine.

Some at the table laughed, while others looked uncomfortable. Nicole felt her heart harden, realising she couldn't continue living like this. For twenty years, she had tried to make the best of her situation, but it was clear that no one appreciated her efforts. Her husband least of all. She glanced at Henri—his face lit up with a charming smile, as if he hadn't just humiliated her—and knew she was done.

Chapter 7

Nicole put the phone to her ear and waited for her Mam to answer. It was only six a.m. in England, but she couldn't wait any longer. After last night's dinner, she had stayed up all night thinking it over and had arrived at the same conclusion. There was no going back.

"Nicole?" Her mother's soft voice came through the line.

"Hi, Mam."

"Nicole!" Diane Robinson's voice brimmed with delight. "How are you?"

"I'm fine, Mam. I miss you."

"I miss you too, baby. The house is so quiet, you know how it is."

"I know. I'm coming home soon."

Whether it was the tone of her voice or just a mother's intuition, Nicole knew her mum immediately sensed something was wrong.

Instead of the excited screech Nicole had expected, her mother paused with heavy concern. "Why? Is everything alright, Nicole?"

"I've had enough, Mam."

"What?" Her mother spluttered. "Nicole... are you talking about Henri?"

"Yes, Mam." Nicole steeled herself, knowing her mother would try to convince her otherwise. She was way past that point.

"Nicole," her mother started, her voice cracking slightly. "Darling, I'll fly over there and talk to him. There has to be another way. I know you've complained about him in the past, but I'm sure it's something we can smooth over. I—"

"There's nothing to discuss, Mam," Nicole said firmly. "He doesn't make me happy. I can't stay anymore. I need to choose me."

"And what about the kids?"

"They'll be fine," she said. "At least, Henri takes good care of them."

"Nicole..."

"I'll call you later, Mam. I wanted you to be the first to know. I'll figure out the details and call you back."

"Nicole, wait, please don't hang up. Please take your time and think about it. You know you have everything you want there with Henri. All your friends here are so envious. Don't rush your decision, that's all I'm asking."

"I have to go now. Speak later, Mam."

Nicole hated confrontations with her mother and felt that Diane didn't fully grasp the gravity of the situation.

After the call, Nicole knew the weight of her decision was pulling her down, but she wasn't changing her mind this time. She descended the stairs with a strange feeling of serenity. Pierre and Lou were already at the dining table, and Nicole initially wanted to tell them but changed her mind at the last second. It was not the time yet.

"Good morning my sweethearts" she greeted cheerfully, taking her seat at the head of the table.

Only Lou responded. "Bonjour Maman."

Pierre kept his head down, absorbed by his phone, and barely acknowledged her presence. Nicole didn't mind. At this point, she was fine with everything. Nicole suspected Henri encouraged this dynamic, but wasn't sure if it was through the material gifts or another means. It broke her heart, but she understood that it was her reality. Like, with many things in this family, she was resigned to her fate. Still, she clung to the hope that beneath the surface, their bond remained intact.

"Good morning, Madame." Mareva appeared with a tray. "Your breakfast."

"Thank you, Mareva."

A few minutes into her breakfast, Henri came down the stairs. He took the seat beside her and, like his son, acted as though she was invisible.

"Good morning," she greeted cheerfully.

She should have hated him for everything that had happened, but surprisingly, she didn't. She blamed herself. It was all her fault for letting so many things slide, and now it was time to fix it.

"Good morning," Henri muttered.

"Good morning, Dad," Pierre chirped. "Sleep well?"

"Slept well, my boy", Henri answered. "Lou, how are you?"

"I'm fine, Dad," Lou replied with a smile. "Thank you."

The table buzzed with light conversation that didn't include her. Henri talked about the business with the kids, and they also shared about school—things she wasn't privy to. It still hurt a little, and as she finished breakfast, she wondered what she had ever done to her kids. Henri, she could understand, but the kids? All she had done was love them unconditionally.

Finally, Henri stood and picked up his briefcase. "I'll see you later tonight," he said, though Nicole knew he was addressing the kids.

"Bye, Dad," they said in unison.

Nicole waited until he was out of the dining area before chasing after him. She caught up to him in the living room, just before he reached the door. "Henri, wait!"

He turned, clearly irritated. "What? I'm late."

"I won't keep you," she said with a smile. "Can I use the car? I really need to go to Floreal to see Lizzy."

"Didn't you just see her recently?"

Nicole sighed, refusing to back down. "Can I use the car?"

"No. I need it. You can find another means of transportation," he said. "Ask Baptiste to take you in Pierre's car."

"Okay." Nicole nodded and watched Henri leave without another word. There was no point in arguing about it. She didn't go back to the dining room to finish her breakfast. Instead, she went upstairs to get ready.

She rushed through her bath and then chose a simple dress and sandals. She arranged for Baptiste to pick her up as soon as possible. This time, she didn't have the energy to appreciate the view of the coast as Baptiste drove her to Floreal. There was only one thing on her mind, and she was trying to stay brave through it all.

Arriving at Lizzy's house, she settled into one of the sofas in her friend's living room, anxious about Lizzy's reaction.

"Nicole." Lizzy, perched on the edge of her sofa, looked concerned. "You're scaring me. What's happening?"

Nicole forced a laugh. "There's nothing to be scared of," she said. "I'm leaving Henri."

Her confession was met with a long stretch of silence, and then Lizzy suddenly embraced her. "Oh, my darling," she murmured softly, taking Nicole's hands in hers. "How do you feel?"

"I should feel sad," Nicole answered, leaning back. "But I feel nothing at all. I don't know why. I guess I haven't fully processed it yet."

"Do you think you aren't sure yet?" Lizzy asked.

She looked her friend straight in the eyes. "Lizzy, I've never been surer of anything in my life!"

A part of her worried her friend would not support her decision, and if there was anything Nicole needed at that moment it was support. Even though Lizzy had been on the receiving end of Nicole's endless list of complaints about her marriage for years, divorce was still a very big deal and it was frowned upon. What made matters worse was she was divorcing a rich and powerful man. It was unheard of!

Lizzy was calmer than usual, but she also had more questions than usual. "What prompted this decision? I know Henri hasn't been the best husband, but you've stayed with him for twenty years."

"I'm just forty, Lizzy. It's time for me to be happy. I'm tired of living like a prisoner in my own house. I want to go back home where I belong."

"Oh, Nicole." Lizzy smiled sadly. "I'm so proud of you. Not many women are brave enough to make this kind of decision. You're so strong."

Nicole sighed in relief. "Thank you. That's all I came to say," she said, rising to her feet. "I have to get home early. Baptiste is waiting outside, so—"

"Shut up." Lizzy prodded her gently. "You're not going anywhere, not if I can help it."

"Let's go to Port Louis. A little shopping might clear our minds, don't you think?"

Nicole knew Lizzy was trying to help, but today, shopping felt trivial, even though it was one of her favourite things to do.

"I'm sorry, Lizzy."

"OK then, let's go to the Dinarobin .Do you remember? We were there nearly every day". Lizzy nudged Nicole's shoulder while bursting into laughter. "You loved the peace and tranquillity of the hotel".

The slight twitch of Lizzy's lips betrayed her cheerful smile. Nicole could easily tell her friend was way more worried than she let on. Nothing could take her mind off of the fact that she was about to leave all of this behind. Leaving Henri was not going to be easy, and even her friend could see that.

Nothing could make her change her mind and after a succession of goodbye hugs from Lizzy, Nicole finally got back into the car and headed back home. Even though her visit had been much shorter than the ride to Floreal, it was worth it.

Baptiste dropped her off in front of the house later that day. She walked slowly to the doorway, relieved to find no one downstairs. She saw Mareva polishing the silver cutlery and quietly crept to the kitchen.

"Madame..."

"Mareva, I wish to discuss something important," Nicole quickly said. Mareva seemed concerned and promptly dropped the cloth in her hand. Nicole sat at the kitchen counter, perched on one of the high stools, her favourite retreat from the world when she needed solace. Mareva moved quietly around the kitchen, preparing chamomile tea, the scent filling the space.

"Merci, Mareva," Nicole whispered as the maid placed two steaming mugs on the counter between them. The older woman stood opposite Nicole, her usually composed expression softening with concern as she observed her mistress's troubled face.

Nicole cradled the warm mug in her hands.

"Do you ever wonder what your life would have been like if you had made different choices?" she asked suddenly, her voice barely above a whisper.

Mareva tilted her head thoughtfully. "Yes Madame. But I learned long ago that dwelling on 'what ifs' only brings sorrow."

Mareva reached across the small space and placed her hand gently over Nicole's trembling fingers. "Perhaps, Madame, it's time you told me everything."

Tears welled up in Nicole's eyes as twenty years of suppressed emotions threatened to overwhelm her. "I was so young and foolish when I married Henri," she began, her voice cracking. "I thought I was getting a fairy tale ending, the handsome prince, the luxurious lifestyle. Instead, I got a golden cage."

Mareva listened intently, her heart aching for the woman who had become more than just her employer over the years. She had watched Nicole transform from a vibrant young bride into a shadow of herself under Henri's oppressive control. She remembered how Nicole's contagious laughter became inaudible soon after her marriage. Her smile sporadic.

The soft ticking of the kitchen clock provided a sombre backdrop as Nicole paused to gather her thoughts. Mareva remained silent.

"I miss my old life," Nicole admitted, her voice thick with emotion. "I miss England and Middlesbrough, my friends, my Mam. Most days, I feel like I don't even recognise myself anymore. Who is this person wearing designer clothes and expensive jewellery? This isn't who I am."

"You are still the same kind-hearted woman who first walked through these doors twenty years ago, Madame".

They stayed in companionable silence for several minutes. Finally, Nicole spoke, her voice steady despite the turmoil inside her.

"Mareva, I need to leave him. I can't keep living this lie. You've been more than just a maid to me," she said softly. "You've been my confidante, my friend, my rock in this stormy sea. I couldn't have survived without you".

"Your friendship has meant more to me than you'll ever know", Mareva replied.

In that quiet room, surrounded by the familiar scents and sounds of the kitchen, Nicole found the courage to start planning her escape from the golden cage she'd called home for twenty years. And Mareva, ever loyal and supportive, vowed to help her every step of the way.

She left the kitchen and headed to her bedroom, breathing a sigh of relief as she shut the door.

"Welcome back, Nicole."

She whirled around to see Henri lounging on the only sofa in the room. He stood slowly, a wry smile on his face. "I was wondering if you'd make it home tonight."

"You scared me." Nicole put a hand to her heart. "You know I went to Lizzy's."

"I don't actually care where you went," he spat. "I know you won't go far. Without me, you'd be stuck in that town of yours. You will never leave me and the life of luxury you have here thanks to me."

Nicole shook her head, wondering how she had coped with this man through the years.

"And I don't care for your rhetoric tonight, Nicole." Henri rolled his eyes. "I'm here to warn you that the next time you pull a stunt like this, I'm sending you back to where you came from. You will respect me under *my* roof."

Her eyes traced his body from his feet right up to his menacing eyes. This was the man she had loved and called her husband for twenty years. This was the man for whom she had left her home.

Back then, she had loved every minute of the 12-hour flight because every minute brought her closer to the love of her life. Now looking into his eyes, there was not a single trace of love. She was convinced, now more than ever, that Henri had never really loved her. Being married to Nicole meant very little to him.

In twenty years, Nicole never stopped loving Henri. Henri never stopped cheating.

Henri was the type of man who wanted to conquer everything and everyone. In hindsight, he didn't treat her any different from how he treated Mareva. To him, everyone in his household was his possession. The only person Henri would ever respect was himself.

"Don't you worry about me," Nicole said with newfound confidence. "I'll leave *your* house very soon."

Henri stomped toward her, stopping just a few feet away. He was close enough for her to see his ocean-blue eyes that had once stolen her heart, but now they left her cold. "And what's that supposed to mean?" he demanded.

"I'm leaving, Henri. I'm going back to Middlesbrough."

His nose wrinkled in disgust. "What for?"

Of course, the great Henri De Marigny couldn't fathom anyone wanting to leave his vast wealth for a simple life. Money was everything to him. If only Nicole had realised he would never love anything or anyone more than he loved money.

"I am leaving," she repeated, her voice stronger. "I'm tired of all this…" she waved the space between them, "I want to be happy."

He threw his head back and laughed. It probably sounded like a joke to him, but she didn't care. She stood patiently, waiting for him to get all his laughter out.

"Wow, that has to be the most hilarious thing you've ever said," he wiped a stray tear from his eyes, still chuckling.

Suddenly, his features got sharper as his expression transformed from amusement to predatory. He looked like a wolf about to devour its prey.

His voice dropped to a low, rumbling tone she had never heard before.

"I dare you."

A heavy silence fell between them as he stared her down. The corners of his eyes wrinkled with amusement, but his lips remained in a thin, hard line. A chill ran up her spine as she struggled to maintain eye contact.

"I assure you," he continued, "you won't last more than a day out there."

He closed the gap between them in one step. "But know this, Nicole *Robinson*," he said, his warm breath blowing in her face, "once you leave this house, you will never come back."

She balled her hands into fists, trying to control the trembling. "I won't."

Henri now bent down until their eyes were level. "You seem to have forgotten where you came from. You have no money… nothing!"

The tension was so heavy her nerves were shot. Unable to take it any longer, she pushed past him and sat on the bed.

"If you're done, you can leave now," she said, hoping she still sounded confident, "I want to go to bed."

Her seemingly nonchalant demeanour finally broke his arrogance. "I'd like to see you survive without me!"

"Thank you, Henri," she said, tucking her legs under the covers, even though she hadn't gotten ready for bed yet.

"You will be on your hands and knees begging me for mercy, just you wait."

"Alright. Goodnight, dear."

Henri growled and stormed off, slamming the door on his way out. It was a small victory, but a victory nonetheless.

As Nicole lay on her bed, her resolve felt stronger than ever. There was no turning back. Finally, she was leaving Henri De Marigny.

Chapter 8

"The only regret in life, is to never make a choice at all."
-James Hauenstein

The day arrived much sooner than she had anticipated. Although she had felt empowered in making her decision, the reality was that she was not in control. Henri had given her a very short deadline. He wanted her out of his house for "betraying" him. So, while it was her choice to leave, it still ended up being his decision as to when she would leave.

Henri was the kind of man who always had to be in charge and have the last word, and though she had come to despise this trait, there was no use in fighting it, all she wanted to do was to get away from him no matter what.

While she was aware that this day was coming, she still awoke with a heavy heart. It wasn't the thought of never seeing Henri again that saddened her, she had come to terms with that already. Rather, it was the fact that she was leaving behind the home and family she had known for the past twenty years.

She reached for her phone on the bedside table. As relieved as she was to finally be free, she still needed a bit of encouragement. The first person Nicole thought of was her mam, so she dialled her number.

"Nicole?" Her mother answered on the first ring. "Nicole, how're you?"

"I'm fine, Mam," Nicole released a shaky breath. "I'm coming home tomorrow."

"Nicole—" her mother began, but the words seemed to catch in her throat. "Honey, I don't think—"

Nicole swallowed painfully, fighting back tears. She needed to sound resolute if she was going to convince her mother that leaving was the right decision. Crying over the phone would prove the opposite.

"Don't worry, Mam, I've been thinking about it for a long time. I'm ready… I know I am."

"Are you sure, Nicole? Are you?"

"I'm sure, Mam," Nicole replied, just managing to end the sentence. "I'll see you soon."

"Okay," her mother said quietly.

Nicole could imagine the embarrassment and ridicule her family would face over this decision, but she could no longer think of others. This was the only life she would ever get to live. Yes, people would probably gossip about her at first, but in time, they'd forget and move on like nothing ever happened. Still, she felt terrible for having to put her family through the shame.

After ending the call she looked around, a faint sound of laughter drifted to her from the hallway. It was Lou's voice.

Now was time to tell her children .She had put it off several times. It was painful, but Nicole didn't think it would matter much to them, which was why she had held back in the first place.

Nicole walked towards the door and into the hallway. The kids weren't in sight, but the laughter grew louder as she followed it to Lou's room. The door was slightly ajar, and Nicole peeked inside. Her children were huddled on the sofa, talking and laughing. Lou was showing Pierre something on her phone.

In an ideal world, Nicole would have walked into the room to joyous greetings, with her kids rushing to her, hugging her, and urging her to sit with them, but Nicole knew that wasn't how it would play out. To confirm her reality, she pushed the door open and stepped inside. "Hello, kids."

Pierre looked up, his expression neutral. "Hi, Mam."

Lou just raised a brow. Her attention was still firmly on her screen. Sadly, this was what Nicole had expected.

"There is something I need to tell you, to you both," Nicole said, her voice wavering. "I am sorry sweethearts. I'm leaving."

Pierre's face remained expressionless. She couldn't tell if he was listening or if he had heard her but just didn't care.

Nicole took a deep breath, her heart pounding. "I'm leaving your father," she clarified.

For a few seconds, the room was silent. Pierre glanced at Lou whose head snapped up, then back at Nicole.

"I don't understand," he said. "What do you mean you're leaving?"

"I'm leaving this marriage, Pierre," Nicole explained, her voice trembling. She had been resolute when making the decision, but now, facing her children, her resolve was cracking, especially with Pierre looking at her like she had betrayed him.

"You're leaving Dad?" Pierre's voice rose in disbelief. "Why? You've been married for over twenty years. What could be so wrong?"

"Maybe you haven't noticed but I'm not happy" Nicole's voice cracked. "This is not how marriage should be."

Although her children were teenagers, she knew this would be difficult for them to understand. However, she didn't want them to believe that this was what a normal marriage looked like.

"So you're leaving because you're not happy?" Pierre's frown deepened.

"Its sound very selfish to me!"

"Pierre!"

"What?" He threw his arms in the air. "Mam, you've been with dad for twenty years. Can't you just stay?"

"I'm not happy," Nicole repeated, her eyes filling with tears. "For years, I've held on. I've tried to stay so you could be happy and comfortable, but I can't do it anymore. I need to protect my sanity before I lose it completely."

"Okay," Pierre said quietly. "I understand, but I'm not coming with you. I don't want to live in England and I need Dad. I need—"

"I'm not asking you to come with me, Pierre. I'm not asking for anything from you."

Even at that moment, hearing that his mother was leaving, her son still chose his father's money over her love. This hurt far worse than the divorce. It took all the strength not to completely break down in front of her children.

She would have never forced them to choose, but she also never thought they would out rightly tell her that they would never choose her.

"Fine!" Pierre growled, and brushed past her shoulder, storming out of the room.

Nicole's heart ached as she watched him leave, feeling the sting of his rejection.

Turning to Lou, Nicole tried to find some comfort. "Darling—" She barely finished before

Lou threw herself into her arms. Nicole wrapped her arms around her daughter and cried with her, unable to hold back any longer.

"I'm sorry, Mam," Lou sobbing uncontrollably. "I'm so sorry."

"I should be the one apologising," Nicole said, trying to comfort Lou. "I'm the one who wasn't brave enough. I tried, but—"

"Mam, you're the bravest woman I know," Lou said, pulling away to look her mother in the eyes. "I see everything, Mam. I'm sorry I haven't been there for you. I feel terrible."

"Oh, my Lou, it's okay. Everything will be alright." Nicole wiped away Lou's tears, ignoring her own. "You don't have to feel obliged to come with me, okay? I understand. You have your school in Paris and with a short flight we will be able to see each other as much as you wish."

"Oh Maman," Lou said, hugging her tightly again. "I've been a terrible daughter."

"No, darling," Nicole said softly.

"Mam, please forgive Pierre. He's just acting out," Lou said. "Dad is just... I'm sure he'll come around."

Nicole kissed Lou's cheek.

"When are you going?"

"Tomorrow darling".

"What?" Lou clung to her. "You're leaving tomorrow?"

Nicole nodded, and Lou burst into new tears. "I thought I still had time with you. I'm going to miss you so much".

The words struck Nicole. She hadn't expected this depth of emotion from Lou, who had grown distant over the years. Her heart swelled with both joy and sorrow, a bittersweet combination.

"I didn't think you'd miss me this much," Nicole admitted. "It warms my heart, Lou, truly."

"How could I not? You're my maman adorée. I will miss you Mam."

Nicole reached out, taking Lou's hand in hers. "Everything will be Ok, darling. I promise."

But the assurance sounded hollow even to her own ears. How could she promise something she wasn't sure of herself?

Nicole had always known this day would come, but she never imagined it would be so difficult. The realisation that Lou cared this much was both heartening and heart breaking. It warmed her to know that her daughter loved her deeply, yet it tore at her soul to think of leaving her behind. "I'm so sorry, Lou," Nicole whispered, kissing the top of her head. "I never wanted to hurt you."

"We better go to sleep now darling it is nearly midnight".

"Bonne nuit Maman," Lou said, her voice barely above a whisper.

"Bonne nuit my darling," Nicole replied, closing the door gently behind her.

As she walked back to her room, Nicole felt the heaviness in her chest ease slightly. Despite the pain of leaving, she found solace in knowing that her decision was understood and supported by her daughter. It was a silver lining in the cloud of uncertainty that loomed ahead, a comforting thought that would guide her through the days to come.

She then thought of having a conversation with Pierre and went to his room. The hallway was quiet, the only sound, Nicole's soft footsteps, as she approached Pierre's room. Her heart pounded in her chest, feeling the gravity of this moment. She paused outside his door, before lifting her hand to knock gently.

"Oui?" Pierre's voice came from within, slightly muffled.

"Can I come in?" Nicole asked.

There was a brief silence before Pierre responded, "Yes, come in."

To her surprise, Pierre wasn't on his phone. Instead, he was sitting on the edge of his bed, looking at her. His blue eyes, so much like his father's, filled with a mixture of curiosity and hurt, perhaps?

She walked over and sat on the edge of his bed. "Pierre…" taking a deep breath. "This isn't easy for me. I want you to know that everything I've done, I've done because I believe it's necessary."

Pierre's expression darkened, and he shook his head. "Necessary? You're leaving us, Mam. How is that necessary?"

"I understand you're upset, Pierre," Nicole said, reaching out to touch his arm, but he pulled away slightly. "And I'm sorry for the pain this is causing you, but sometimes, we have to make difficult choices."

Pierre stood up abruptly, pacing the room. "You're choosing yourself over us, over your family. Do you even realise how much this hurts?"

"I do, Pierre. More than you know, but staying in a situation that makes me unhappy wouldn't be fair to any of us. You'll understand when you're older."

He stopped pacing and turned to face her, his eyes blazing. "Why are you telling me this now? Why not earlier?"

"Because I needed to see you alone," Nicole explained, her voice breaking slightly. "I wanted to ask you something very important."

Pierre crossed his arms over his chest, still visibly upset but listening intently. "What is it?"

Nicole stood up, moving closer to him. She placed her hands on his shoulders, looking deeply into his eyes. "Promise me, Pierre, that you will look after your sister. She needs you, especially now."

Pierre's defences seemed to soften slightly, and he nodded slowly. "I promise, Mam. Of course I'll take care of her."

A wave of relief washed over Nicole, easing the tightness in her chest. She pulled him into a hug, holding him close for a moment before pulling back. "Thank you, Pierre. That means more to me than you can imagine."

She stepped back. "I love you, Pierre. Always remember that." Pierre didn't say it back, but the slight nod and the way his eyes softened told her he understood. Nicole forced a small smile. With one last affectionate look, she turned and walked towards the door.

Closing the door softly behind her, Nicole leaned against the wall in the hallway, letting the tears flow freely. The weight of her decision pressed heavily on her heart, but knowing that Pierre would be there for Lou brought her some comfort. As she made her way back to her room, Nicole reflected on the conversation. Pierre's hurt was palpable, yet she saw a flicker of understanding in his eyes; a glimmer of hope that someday, he would see why she had to leave.

The next morning she felt the guilt of not telling Mareva earlier, but the decision had been made hastily. She found Mareva in the veranda, and as soon as Mareva saw the luggage, her face fell.

"Madame?" Mareva asked, glancing at the bags. "I didn't know you were travelling."

Even as she said this, Nicole could tell that Mareva had already figured out what was going on, but had hoped it wasn't true.

"I'm leaving, Mareva," Nicole said softly, walking up to her and pulling her into a hug. "I'm leaving Henri."

Mareva's shoulders slumped and began to shake.

"I'm so sorry," Nicole whispered, as Mareva silently sobbed.

This was the first time she had ever seen her shed tears and it broke her heart that she was the reason. They had developed a camaraderie, finding ways to make life bearable.

In those few minutes, she wondered how Mareva would survive. Surely, with her gone and the sting of divorce, Henri would be worse than he had ever been. She couldn't even imagine how he would treat Mareva now.

She couldn't say "Everything will be okay" because that would be a lie. If anything, Mareva's life would be much harder from now on.

Nicole hated herself for having to break so many hearts for the sake of her own happiness. Maybe her children would be okay after a few days, but Mareva would be at the receiving end of all the frustration in the house from Henri and them.

"You have to go now, Madame."

"Mareva—"

"We will be okay," she smiled sadly. "I—I will be okay."

"I'm so sorry, Mareva. I will call you, I promise."

Mareva was now her usual calm self. "Madame, I hope you find the peace you deserve. It is not your fault."

Mareva sighed deeply, "I will be okay. I have Baptiste, our children and grandchildren. I made the choice to work for Monsieur because I love my family. You are making the choice to leave because you love your family."

Mareva's words meant so much to Nicole.

"Thank you, Mareva, I will miss you. I'm not sure I would have lasted this long without you."

Without another word, Nicole turned and walked out of the kitchen. The moment Nicole stepped out of the De Marigny villa for the last time, the weight of her departure pressed heavily on both women. Mareva stood at the door, her hands clasped tightly in front of her apron, knuckles white with unspoken emotion. Her usual composed demeanour faltered as tears welled up in her eyes, blurring the sight of Nicole walking toward the waiting car. For two decades, they had been more than mistress and maid… they had been confidantes, silent supporters to eachother.

Nicole paused by the gate, turning back to look at Mareva one final time, staring at the familiar figure framed in the doorway. Mareva nodded faintly.

Baptiste was waiting outside by the car and helped her load the luggage into the boot. Lou insisted on accompanying her to the airport, but Nicole gently refused. "No, Lou. It will be too hard to say goodbye if you come. I'll go alone, but I'll call you as soon as I land, okay?"

"But will you come back?" Lou asked, clinging to her.

"This can't be the last time you'll ever come here, Mam. It just can't be."

Nicole wanted to say that she doubted Henri would let her return, but she didn't want to cause Lou more pain.

"I'm sure I will, but if you want to see me anytime, I'll book a flight for you Ok?"

Lou nodded and hugged her mother once more. "I love you, Mam."

Nicole kissed Lou's hair and pulled away. "Take care, Lou. Be strong!" she said, sliding into the car.

Baptiste drove away and Nicole watched as Mareva was standing a few steps behind Lou. As they left the property, Nicole rolled down the window and waved at the two of them. Pierre watched from his bedroom's window. His heart was aching.

Chapter 9

"I am strong enough to live without you, strong enough and I quit crying long enough".-Cherr

Henri arrived home later than usual. The past few months at work had been busy as he diversified his business, leaving him exhausted every day however Nicole wasn't naïve; she noticed how often he was in Mahébourg and how late he returned home, claiming to be attending business meetings.

He walked through the living room and straight to the dining area. There was a cafeteria at work, but he liked to eat fresh meals, so he always made sure not to miss breakfast and dinner at home.

"Welcome back, Monsieur," Mareva greeted as soon as he stepped into the dining room.

"Bring me my dinner, will you?" he requested, sitting at the table. As he waited for Mareva to bring his food, his phone started to ring. Henri reached for it. It was Bernard. "Hello."

"Henri, where are you?"

He rubbed his temple. "Home, why? Why is it so noisy?"

"I have just arrived in Flic en Flac. Let's go out."

"I don't know," Henri said." I've had a long day."

"Come on," Bernard pressed. "I want to make an announcement. Gilles and Xavier will be here too. It's important."

"Okay," Henri answered curiously. "I'll be there within the hour."

As he contemplated whether he should eat his dinner or not, Mareva arrived with a tray of delicious food. It was grilled sea bass with a lemon herb sauce, accompanied by a side of roasted vegetables, including stuffed bell peppers, zucchini, and cherry tomatoes. Mareva had also included freshly baked bread, which he had to have with almost every meal, and a small salad with mixed greens and a light vinaigrette dressing, which added a refreshing touch.

Deciding not to waste such a delectable meal, he decided to eat a little. His friends would have to wait. Even though he was hard on her sometimes, he couldn't deny Mareva was a good cook and the main reason he enjoyed his meals at home.

Of course, he would never admit this to her. He didn't believe in being soft with the help.

Mareva soon walked in with a bottle of wine to complement his sea bass and he immediately barked an order, frightening her.

"Go and tell Baptiste to sit in the car and wait for me. I still have somewhere to be."

"Yes, Monsieur Henri." She replied hurriedly, and dashed out of the room, leaving the bottle unopened.

"Dad?"

Henri looked up to see Lou standing on the stairs. She had an envelope in her hand.

"Hi," he greeted.

Lou climbed down the rest of the stairs and came to a stop in front of him. "Here." She held out the envelope.

"What is this?" he asked, taking it from her. Instead of responding, Lou ran up the stairs.

Henri frowned and tore the envelope open. A letter fell out. "It better not be a bad report," he called out after her, even though she couldn't hear him.

Henri,

By the time you're reading this, I'll be long gone. I think you will agree that things have not been good between us for a very long time. As I told you the other night, I can't do this anymore.
I know you told me to leave your house today and finally, I have the courage to choose me. And don't you worry, I won't come back. I'll get a lawyer and start the divorce process.
Maybe we will see each other one day, or maybe we won't. Either way, I hope we both find peace. I will always wish you the best for having given me the greatest gift in life, our children. I hope you will take good care of them and give them the life they deserve as De Marignys.

Goodbye, Henri.

Nicole Robinson.

Henri scanned the letter again, then folded it neatly and laid it on the table. Although he didn't feel bad or upset, he suddenly had an intense need to be around his friends. He rushed to his feet, grabbed his phone, and walked out of the house. Baptiste was already waiting, and the car zoomed off as soon as he settled in.

He arrived in Flic en Flac after a few minutes. Flic en Flac, as a popular town on the west coast of Mauritius, was alive with activity, especially at this late hour. The beachfront was lined with restaurants and lively bars, all illuminated by strings of lights.

As Baptiste navigated the car through the seafront, Henri observed groups of people laughing and chatting outside the trendy cafes and bars. The crowd was a mix of locals and tourists, all enjoying the relaxed, festive vibe for which Flic en Flac was known.

Finally, they pulled up in front of a chic, modern restaurant with a large outdoor seating area. The place was abuzz with activity, the tables filled with people enjoying the warmth of the evening. Henri spotted his friends at a corner table, seated on bar stools, tapping their feet to the music, already deep in conversation, their laughter carrying over the ambient sounds of music and chatter.

His friends welcomed him to the table with eager back slaps and excited laughs. He loved hanging out with his friends, and right now, he would rather be here than anywhere else.

"What's the occasion?" he asked as soon as he sat down. "It's almost ten p.m., guys." His friends had already ordered drinks, and the table was filled with several alcohol bottles and tumblers. He poured himself a drink. "So what's up?"

"Bernard called us out for the same reason he called you," Gilles Arnault said. "Apparently, he has news."

They all turned to Bernard. "What's so important you have us all out of the house this late?"

"Well, I was feeling sorry for myself," Bernard said. "And I decided to call you all out so you can feel sorry for me too and maybe it would make me feel better."

Bernard poured himself another drink and took a big gulp. "Claire is pregnant."

They all whistled and burst into laughter at Bernard's frustrated confession.

"Isn't this wonderful news?" Xavier Meyers teased. "I mean, children are a blessing, aren't they?"

Bernard gulped down the rest of his drink. "I mean, yes, but not after three."

Henri refilled Bernard's glass.

"At this point, I think Claire is trying to build an empire," Xavier added.

Bernard glared at him.

"Seriously," Xavier continued, "it's not that dreadful. Trudi and I are still trying for more kids."

"After two?" Henri asked. "What more do you want?"

"It won't hurt," Xavier shrugged. "Trudi wants it way more than I do, but I'm not complaining. Are two kids enough for you? What's Nicole saying about that?"

Henri slammed the tumbler on the table. "My word is law in my home. If I say I want more kids, Nicole has no options."

The men exchanged surprised glances, but Henri continued. "And two kids is enough for me, thank you. I'd rather not have more kids with Nicole if I can help it."

What he left out was that he couldn't have any more kids with Nicole even if he wanted to because she had left him. The more he thought about it the more it infuriated him. How dare she leave him? After all he had done for her? How dare she embarrass him in such a manner?

"Isn't that a little harsh?" Bernard asked.

"I'm sorry, it's the truth." Henri shrugged. "I'm not one to water down the truth."

"Well, I don't think Nicole would feel good about that if she hears it, that's all I'm saying," Bernard insisted. "She's your wife."

Henri's grip tightened around the glass. He wanted to tell them not to call her that. She was not his wife. She was just a poor, foolish, ungrateful woman who had decided to punish him for all the good he had done for her and her family.

"Do you think Claire would feel good to hear you're not happy about her new pregnancy?" Henri shot back, and the table melted into another round of laughter.

"Touché." Bernard raised his glass and brought it to his lips.

"No hard feelings." Henri reached out to pat Bernard's shoulder.

At this moment, he couldn't keep it in anymore. Maybe it was the liquor he had just downed on a nearly empty stomach, but he suddenly felt the urge to just tell them and get it over with.

"Nicole and I are no longer together," he blurted out as he poured himself yet another drink.

Xavier spat out his wine. "What?"

The men looked at each other and back at him, waiting for him to tell them he was joking. It had been less than a week since they'd all hung out at Le Royal Palm and of course, this news shocked them.

Bernard leaned forward in his seat and lowered his voice. "What happened?"

"I don't know." Henri shrugged. "I just arrived home today and found this stupid letter she left. She wants a divorce."

For the first time all night, the table fell dead silent. Henri and Nicole had been married the longest, so this was not the kind of news they thought they'd be receiving.

Although Henri kept trying to convince himself he was unbothered, he was fuming on the inside. Not only had he dared her to leave, he had even given her a date to scare her. What he didn't expect was for her to actually leave, and do so the day before the date he threatened to kick her out.

After a few minutes, Bernard finally had the courage to be the honest one of the bunch. "I mean, it's not really surprising. We all saw it coming, didn't we?"

The men nodded in agreement.

Henri frowned. He raised his eyes from his glass and scanned his friend's faces. "What do you mean you saw it coming?"

They cowered under his gaze, but Bernard felt particularly confident. "It was obvious you weren't treating her well. The rest of us talk about it all the time."

Henri sat up straight. "Oh, is that right?"

"Come on, man, you've got to admit it. Even you know it's true."

As much as Henri wanted to lash out at his friend and assert his dominance, Bernard's honesty caused a little introspection. He wouldn't lie to himself and say he loved Nicole. Maybe he did at the beginning, but the feelings fizzled out so fast after she moved in with him as his wife. He started to find faults in everything she did and got irritated more often than not. He had acquired her the same way he acquired properties and businesses he found lucrative.

He had met her at a restaurant in England and immediately fell for her beauty. She was indeed radiant, young and he felt the need to possess her. However, just like the property he bought and got tired of, he quickly grew tired of his new wife. She started to bear children, and the beauty he had been so attracted to, became diluted with age. Nicole was still pretty but had lost that radiance that had initially attracted him.

All this wasn't new to him. However, it was surprising that his friends had noticed this for years. He thought their marriage was good, at best. He didn't know their problems had been so obvious for others to see, which only angered him more. This meant the De Marigny name had been running through the gossip circles for years, and it was all because of that woman.

His friends were looking at him expectantly, so he smirked. "Well, I stopped loving her years ago, but I don't think I mistreated her."

Bernard's brows went up so high they almost touched his hairline. "You don't see it?"

"Women want to feel loved," Xavier said, concerned.

Henri clicked his tongue, shook his head and glared at him. "Says the man who has two girlfriends. Meyers, please!"

"What?" Xavier shrugged dismissively as the men laughed. "Talking about women, these ladies came in over half an hour ago and have been eyeing our table. What do you guys think?"

"Where?" The men twisted their necks to get a good view of the women. "First table by the window."

The ladies in question were both beautiful and seemed classy. Totally Henri's type. The blonde was sporting a sleek ponytail and a red bodycon dress that fell right above her knees. The brunette seemed to be more conservative in a white jumpsuit. She reminded him so much of Nicole that he immediately focused all his attention on the blonde.

"How about we invite them over for a drink?" he suggested. "But the blonde one is mine."

"Oh, look who's ready for a rebound," Xavier jested. "We can just buy them a drink and then I will have to go. It's getting late."

"What?" Henri eyed his friend. "Why the rush to go home! The night is still young. Invite them over."

Henri downed his drink and signalled to the waiter to order a fresh round. Xavier already gestured to the ladies, and they were coming over.

It wasn't a rebound like his friend had suggested. Henri had been indulging in activities like this for most of his marriage to Nicole. The only difference was he was more discreet back then. Now that she was gone, he was ready to throw caution to the wind.

The two ladies stopped right in front of their table, eyeing the empty bottles of expensive liquor that littered their table.

"Hello, gentlemen," the brunette said, batting her eyelashes in what looked like an attempt to flirt.

Henri ignored her and locked eyes with the blonde, reaching out for her hand. "Come here, you pretty thing. Why don't you sit beside me while we wait for food, hmm?"

She pushed past her seemingly inexperienced friend and lowered herself into the space beside him and Moreau. He boldly placed his hand on her thigh, pulling her closer. Tonight, he was going to forget about the English woman who had taken up space in his life for twenty years and focus on the hot, young blonde beside him.

~~~~~

The soft click of the front door echoed through the grand, silent halls of the De Marigny Villa as Henri stepped inside. The cool night air followed him momentarily before he shut the door firmly behind him, cutting off the faint hum of crickets and distant waves. He paused, loosening his tie and glancing at his watch: half past midnight. Late by most standards, but not unusual for him these days.

Henri frowned slightly as he noticed light spilling out from under the living room door. His children were still awake? At this hour? He had spent the evening dining with colleagues at one of Mauritius' finest restaurants, enjoying rare moments of genuine camaraderie without the suffocating presence of Nicole hovering nearby or casting disapproving looks across the table. It should have been a relaxing end to an exhausting week of business meetings and strategic planning sessions. Yet here he was, returning home to find that even in her absence, Nicole's influence lingered like a ghost haunting every corner of his meticulously designed estate.

Henri strode into the living room with purposeful steps. There they were: Pierre sprawled on the couch scrolling aimlessly through his phone, while Lou sat curled up in an armchair reading what appeared to be some romance novel. Neither looked up immediately when he entered.

"Children", Henri began sharply, "it is a bit late for either of you to be awake."

Lou finally lifted her gaze from the book, meeting his eyes briefly before rolling hers dramatically skyward. She marked her page carelessly with a finger and rose slowly to her feet, deliberately taking her time gathering her things. Her movements were slow and exaggerated, each action laced with barely concealed resentment. As she passed him on her way out, she shot him a pointed side-eye glance that spoke volumes about her feelings toward him; a mix of bitterness, anger, and something else he couldn't quite place, perhaps disappointment.

Henri watched her go. He knew why she resented him; it wasn't difficult to figure it out, but how could she blame him? He hadn't forced Nicole out; if anything, he had done everything within reason to keep their marriage intact. In fact, hadn't he given her everything she ever wanted? Wealth, status, beautiful children... What more could she possibly desire?

Pierre remained seated casually on the couch, seemingly oblivious to the tension thickening the air around them.

"Pierre," Henri addressed his son, who reluctantly dragged his attention away from whatever digital distraction consumed him. "Did you say you need money?"

Pierre blinked lazily, lowering his phone onto his lap. "Yes, I need to buy clothes," he replied nonchalantly, as if purchasing new attire every month was perfectly normal behaviour for someone barely out of adolescence.

"Clothes?" Henri echoed sceptically. "Fine," Henri acquiesced curtly. "I'll transfer the money to your account first thing in the morning." Without waiting for further acknowledgment, Pierre nodded absently and stood, stretching before shuffling towards the staircase leading upstairs leaving Henri alone in the emptiness of his own empire.

For several long minutes, Henri stood rooted to the spot, staring blankly ahead. The house felt eerily vacant despite its opulent furnishings and sprawling layout. Each room was full of memories both cherished and painful. The laughter shared between family dinners, tense arguments whispered behind closed doors, quiet mornings spent sipping coffee overlooking manicured gardens.

Henri sank onto the nearest sofa, leaning back against plush cushions. He tilted his head upward, gazing at the intricately moulded ceiling above. Deep breaths filled his lungs. He felt a void, an ache until now to him unknown. Nicole's departure loomed large over everything. Though initially blindsided by her decision, Henri quickly believed that she had brought this upon herself. Hadn't she known what marrying into wealth entailed? Didn't she understand the sacrifices required to maintain appearances, uphold traditions, and fulfil expectations?

Henri switched off the lights as he ascended the stairs. He moved silently through the darkness of his home. Reaching his bedroom, he closed the door behind him.

Chapter 10

"I will survive. I've got my life to live and all my love to give and I will survive".
-Gloria Gaynor

Nicole's lips stretched into a wide smile as the morning rays of the sun entered her window. She had only been home for three weeks, but she was already happier than she had been in Mauritius over the past years.

It wasn't even seven yet, but there was a flurry of activity outside as people went about their morning duties. This was life. This was Middlesbrough!

Her room was still as tiny as she remembered it and her ceiling felt lower than it was before, but she was proud to call it her own. This was the room she grew up in. This was her home. For the first time in years, she felt like she belonged.

She slipped out of bed, when she heard shuffling coming from the kitchen.

"Mam?"

Nicole walked out of the room and headed downstairs to see what was going on in the kitchen. Her mother bent over the cooker preparing her special breakfast. This had been Nicole's morning routine every day since the day she got back.

"Oh, Mam." Nicole hugged Diane. "Why do you work so much? I can do this. You rest."

"No." Diane swatted Nicole's hand away when she tried to take the spatula. "You don't know how much I love doing this. It's been so long since I had any company in this house. Since your Dad died this house have been far too quiet."

Nicole raised her hands in surrender and sat on the stool observing her mother. There was no marble kitchen counter. Here in the council estate, marble was considered a luxury.

"Well, you're about to get tired of me because I'm here to stay," Nicole reminded her.

"You're welcome to stay for as long as you want, sweetheart," her mother answered, piling the bacon onto a plate. "Here!" She stretched the plate towards her.

"Thank you, Mam."

"So…" Diane grabbed her own plate and sat across from her. "Are you going to send the divorce papers to Henri?"

Nicole had met with a lawyer just the previous morning and asked him to draw up divorce papers. However, she quickly learned that the whole process would take a minimum of three months. First, she had to submit a divorce application which would take anywhere from ten days to a month. She needed a few documents from Henri in order to complete the application.

"Well?" Diane probed.

"Actually, the lawyer explained that I needed to file an application. What makes matters more complicated is that we have children and one is a minor. I will need some documents from Henri to complete the application."

"Have you spoken to him?"

"I'll call him later today."

Nicole could sense Diane eyeing her suspiciously, but she chose to focus on her breakfast. She loved being home, but she was certainly not a fan of all the serious questions over breakfast.

Initially, she thought the divorce would be a quick and easy process because both she and Henri wanted it. However, it was more complicated than that. Having never been through a divorce before, she had no idea what she was walking into, but she was still determined to see it through.

Her mother seemed to be more bothered than she was.

"Nicole baby, I respect your decision," Diane said. "But you have to think about it properly and be sure this is what you want to do. Once you send those papers to him, it's really over."

"It was over the day I left Mauritius, Mam. No, actually it's been over for years now, and I've just been holding on. Henri doesn't love me anymore. He hasn't even called me since I left the house. I'm surprised he hasn't even sent his own divorce papers yet. He really doesn't care about me, so there's nothing to think about."

When her mother didn't say anything, Nicole kept quiet and fixed her attention back to the breakfast in front of her. Today was going to be a good day. She had plans to go around town, especially to walk to the Transporter Bridge, just to re-live scenes from her childhood with her dad. She wanted to see how much Linthorpe Road had changed. She wanted to walk barefoot through Stewart Park, just as when she was little, and went there with dad.

The only downside was that she still hadn't found the courage to call Melanie and Jen. She had been looking forward to seeing them, but now that she was here, she was ashamed. She knew she had offended them terribly by not phoning over the years and didn't know how to make contact again.

Suddenly, her phone rang. She rushed to the living room to get it, thinking Mel and Jen had heard of her return, and decided to reach out first.

Her smile widened when she saw the name on her screen. "Lou!"

"Hi, Mam."

Nicole had remained in constant communication with Lou ever since she left, and it was one of the many things that made her happy. Lou used to never call her before when she was at school in France, but now they spoke almost every day.

Seeing as her mam was still busy, she decided to head up to the room for some privacy.

"Sweetheart, I'm glad you called. How are you?"

"I'm fine. Pierre and I are going back to school in Paris next week. Is there a way I can see you?"

Nicole's heart almost melted. "I can book a flight for you right now, honey, that's not a problem. But you'd have to confirm with your father first."

Lou lowered her voice to a barely audible whisper. "What if he says no? He's been acting weird lately. He has a new girlfriend now and spends all his time with her."

"Oh." Nicole paused to analyse how she felt about this news. She expected anger, sadness, and even jealousy, but none of that came. Her heart felt free. It was a great feeling. However, she was worried about her children.

"Who is she?" Nicole asked.

"Some girl," Lou grumbled. "We don't see them for long. They just come and go."

"Some girl?" Nicole echoed.

"Yes, Mam, girl! She's barely older than Pierre and acts even less mature. I wonder what Dad was thinking."

Although she felt nothing for Henri, it felt totally good that her daughter disliked the new girl.

"I'll call your dad today and ask him if it's okay for you to come. Okay?"

"Okay, thanks, Mam. I love you."

"I love you too, darling."

Nicole heard voices in the living room as she ended the call and wondered who had come to visit her mother this early. Just as she was thinking it, the door to her bedroom swung open and two familiar faces marched in with frowns on their faces.

Her jaw dropped. Staring back at her were the very women she had been hesitant to call.

Jen marched forward and slapped Nicole's shoulder. "Why didn't you tell us you were back, you silly girl?"

Nicole burst into laughter and got up, recovering from her total shock. "Jen! Melanie!" She pulled the girls into her arms and embraced them. "I missed you both so much."

"Did you?" Jen pouted. "Because we are upset with you. You never returned our calls."

Nicole was guilty of that. She wasn't going to act like she didn't know what they were talking about. Years into her marriage, she started to feel a lot of resentment toward those who had indirectly convinced her to marry Henri because he was rich and handsome. The resentment caused her to stop responding to their texts and taking their calls. However, by the time she realised no one was to blame but herself, it was too late to call them back.

"I'm sorry," she said genuinely to her friends. "I missed you girls so much, I really did. But I was skeptical about calling you back."

"We never stopped thinking about you," Melanie said softly. "We always asked Diane about you and were happy to know you were fine even if you wouldn't speak to us."

"What happened, Nicole?" Jen asked, sitting on the bed. Mel joined her.

It amazed Nicole how they managed to make themselves so comfortable with her, even after her silence for all these years.

"I was going through it," Nicole explained. "My Prince Charming wasn't really a prince, after all."

"Tell me about it," Melanie grunted. "I'm also divorced."

Nicole started to relax, enough to tell them all about her life as Mrs. De Marigny. These were her friends. They wouldn't judge her.

After she told them her story, the girls wrapped their arms around her again. "His loss!"

"I know." Nicole nodded. "That's why I came home."

"You know what?" Jen said. "Get dressed and let's talk about it over a cup of coffee. I want to know all about your beautiful children too."

"Sounds great." Nicole nodded eagerly and grabbed her handbag, and they were off for a coffee in town.

~~~

Later that night, Nicole, relaxing on her bed, felt more at peace than she had in years. The day had gone wonderfully, just as she had imagined when she woke up that morning. Now that she and her childhood friends were on good terms, she knew Middlesbrough would only get better for her.

It was already ten p.m., so Henri was either asleep or not far off. Nicole decided to call him regardless. She wished she didn't have to, but her desire to see Lou was far more important. She dialled Henri's number and put the phone to her ear. He picked up on the first ring.

"Hi, it's Nicole."

After a brief pause, Henri scoffed, "I know, I haven't deleted your number yet."

"I'll need some documents from you so I can submit the divorce application," she asserted. "Please send them to me as soon as possible."

She heard his faint sigh, which was quite unusual. What was even more concerning was how soft his voice was as he spoke to her.

"Is that all?" he asked.

"One more thing…"

"Yes?"

"Lou wants to see me before she goes back to school. I can book her flight tomorrow, but I told her I'd check with you first. Is that okay?"

"Yes." Henri sighed. "You can book her ticket, it's okay. I'll just—"

"That's all," Nicole cut him off. She had not called him to have a conversation about anything else. "Goodnight, Henri," she said and hung up. It felt good that her heart wasn't slapping against her chest with anxiety.

Henri no longer had an insane hold on her. She was free, finally. She texted Lou the outcome of the conversation and laid back down. Tomorrow, she would send Henri a list of all the documentation he needed to provide for them to submit the divorce application.

Tomorrow marked the beginning of Nicole's 'rest of her life', and she would make sure to live it well this time around.

Epilogue

"What doesn't kill me, makes me stronger"
-F.Nietzsche

A year had passed since Nicole's life changed into something more quiet, more simple, and infinitely more meaningful. She sat on the small sofa of her living room in Middlesbrough, sipping tea as the autumn approached, surrounded by photos of her children and mementos from her journey.

A freshly baked lemon drizzle cake filled the house with a scent that gave her a sense of belonging. Her heart swelled with gratitude for this new chapter but ached with longing too. She missed her children deeply, especially Pierre, whose absence pained her greatly.

It had been a heart-breaking year. Guilt shadowed her days, a reminder of how she'd left her children behind. Was it selfish? Was it irresponsible?

She battled with these questions during sleepless nights but as time went on, she realised she hadn't abandoned them; she had freed herself, and perhaps, in doing so, given them permission to find their own paths.

Slowly, the constant apprehension and humiliation that once defined her existence dissolved, leaving room for calm and clarity. Nicole knew she'd made the right decision; not just for herself, but for everyone involved. Her decision hadn't been perfect; it came with pain, sacrifice, and uncertainty. However, it also brought peace, purpose, and love, and for Nicole, that was enough. She called her experience a learning curve and with that, she grew stronger.

Nicole found solace in volunteering at a charity shop in town discovering the joy in helping others. A sense of fulfilment she'd never known before. Now she is laughing freely again. She allows herself to be Nicole Robinson.

Lou visits often. Their bond has grown stronger than ever, free of the tension of Mauritius. On crisp weekends, they stroll through Albert Park, arms linked, sharing stories and laughter.

Pierre, however, remains distant. He graduated and began working alongside Henri, quickly climbing the ranks within the family empire. He juggles girlfriends and revels in the "lark mirror" of wealth and power. Pierre, to this day, hasn't visited her. Each unanswered phone call and ignored text message hurt her. Yet she hold onto hope that someday, he might understand why she chose freedom over fear.

Nicole wraps herself in a brand new scarf gifted by her dear friends, the vibrant colours of Middlesbrough emblazoned proudly across its fabric. They head together to the Riverside Stadium. The air gentle, the seagulls calling over the North Sea and everything feels right.

Meanwhile, in Mauritius, Mareva and Baptiste continue serving Monsieur Henri. They need to.

Mareva's sacrifices were worth it. With her savings and help from their sons, they purchased a house with a sturdy roof and enough space for their growing family. For the first time, Mareva could live under a safe roof, surrounded by all her loved ones. The shack eventually became a distant memory. She now knows that life is the most precious thing of all. She speaks to Nicole often over the phone, their conversations brimming with warmth and nostalgia. Their friendship enduring despite the distance and becoming an everlasting bond.

In Tamarin another woman has taken Nicole's place—a young woman, wearing red lipstick.

Acknowledgments

I have to start by thanking my dear husband for his patience and precious support, from reading early drafts to giving me advice on the book cover and throughout the long evenings and nights spent writing.

I am deeply grateful to my cherished friends Rosie and Jim Barrett for their tremendous enthusiasm and invaluable advice that made this book possible.

To my wonderful friend Denise, many thanks for sharing memories of her life in South Africa and for my better understanding of the colonisation and Apartheid system.

A heartfelt thank you to Pauline, Peter (Pip) Jones and their family.

I would like to thank my dear friend Linda for sharing her fond recollections of her days in Kenya.

I extend my sincere appreciation to the author Chris Wood for his advice and motivation.

To my friends in Mauritius, thank you!

My gratitude to Manuel Quintana, for his hard work in editing my book.

Thank you Holly for the amazing book cover.

As ever, I am immensely grateful to my parents, my family and my loving friends Marinella, Anastasia, Amanda, Oscar, Pam and Richard Allen for encouraging the publishing of my books.

About the author

Annabella Baker was born in Italy of Austrian descendants.

She is British-Italian, speaks seven languages and lives in Northumberland, England, with her husband and their three Labrador Retrievers.

Passionate of French and Hungarian literature Annabella self-published four of her fictional novellas.

Annabella is a tour guide who also has, for many years, worked as a flight attendant. Writing is one of her hobbies.

She lived in Paris, Budapest, Belgium and Mauritius among other places.

Printed in Dunstable, United Kingdom